Dave

CARBON
AWAKENING

Brother you are amazing so happy you are part of my life!

All my love

BEN WAY

Thank you to my slightly crazy, amazing family for giving me the journey I needed to write this book: to my mum, Caroline; my dad, Christopher; my sister, Hermione; my brothers, Theo and Monty; my niece, Venice; and my nephew, Octavius. It may have not been the easiest journey, but I would change nothing, and I love you all.

Thank you to the amazing best-selling writer and editor Nancy Osa for turning my drafts, ideas, and vision into beautiful words.

PROLOGUE

Dark clouds part. Centered in a frame of blackness, a radiant orb pulses, an eclipse of gold come to life. It dances in hot breath as the first measured steps of a symphony climb—woodwinds meeting strings—and voices rise.

The fiery core parts to admit a metal wand, one end shining white with hot sand. Flames embrace it with fingers of dawn and sunset, the heat seeming to push the musical chorus ever higher, notes terracing in rounds of glory.

The wand retreats, pulls liquid light into the room, into reality, cooling its mass to an undulating orange. The shimmering oval rocks on a bed of pure color, carries shards of sea and sky back to the small sun, into which it thrusts and parries, melting into beauty and shyly backing away again.

The haunting melody soars, escorting the glow and sweep of the long wand through mid air. This motion nudges its bright passenger to curve more, bend less, until—at last—a sphere is born, shifting from hot yellow to deep amber and into ribbons of cobalt, verdigris, indigo. It rests, round, dazzling, strong, fragile. Perfect… or nearly so.

Not good enough, *she thinks.*

In one decisive move, the weight of shade and imperfection topples the globe, draws it down, down through hot air to meet cold ground. Its green–blues and violets and stunning refraction succumb as shrapnel, shattering the night—a sound and vision so complete that the music of men and fire dwindles to whispers, only whispers.

PART I

WASHINGTON (AP) – CALIFORNIA SECESSION
PROMPTS U.S. SANCTIONS

> *California's landslide vote to secede from the U.S.
> earned swift condemnation and, now, severe economic
> restrictions from President Grubb's administration.
> Citing the state's resistance to the U.S.-prompted war
> with Mexico...*

SACRAMENTO (AP) – OREGON, WASHINGTON, NEVADA
ALLY WITH CALIFORNIA

SACRAMENTO (AP) – ARIZONA FOLLOWS SUIT TO
JOIN WESTERN LAND CORE

WASHINGTON – PRESIDENT GRUBB TO ASSUME
SECOND TERM, SELL STATE LANDS

> *In a win for voting restrictions, President Grubb
> will remain in office despite a second loss of the
> popular vote. Wednesday he announced his intent to
> "corporatize" a handful of Western states...*

CHAPTER 1

August 15, 2028

Jennifer Peterson removed her safety glasses and thick, leather gloves and set them on the blowing bench next to her tools. She took in the glittering mess of glass shards at her feet and sighed. Not every finished piece was worth keeping. Still, ego battled will before she'd let one go. Each break served to remind her of some past letdown, not the successes that followed. *Negativity bias sucks*, she thought.

Maybe she took these things too hard, for their effects never seemed to fully fade from her memory. Failure didn't just produce an insight or a gut sensation, she mused. It formed a mouthful, a poison you dared not swallow. It had a taste.

As Jennifer swept up the broken glass in time to the choral music playing in the studio, she recalled one of her most indelible failures, one she'd recently related to a mechanical teammate. It had happened back before the Western split, not long after her homeland had fallen under the sway of anti-intellectuals. She'd been a doctoral student, distracted by pregnancy and her studies, and she hadn't seen the full force of the tsunami coming.

>>> <<<

Jennifer had begun the presentation with her usual confidence—a sort of geek hubris that sprang from possessing relevant data and the foresight with which to use it. The panel might have been forgiven for discounting her potential, given her elfin charm, but her qualifications could not be disputed. An impressive string of letters after her name evidenced milestones in biology, genetics, and computer science conferred by MIT, Chicago, Stanford. And yet, as she spoke, the skeptics grumbled. Any doubts about the slight-framed, pale-skinned, blonde-haired researcher's grasp of her topic would have to spring from bias, not reason.

The darkened assembly room grew increasingly restive with murmured comments and bodies shifting in seats. Jennifer attempted to quell the gathering storm. "These facts are nothing new," she asserted from the podium on the lighted dais. "They're not in question. Machines *will* surpass our intelligence. Soon. What I'm proposing is that we solve the problem of how to use human values to guide their abilities before trouble can arise."

She was heartened to see some nods from the panel of would-be patrons. But then the moderator for the group spoke up.

"Your so-called facts are, indeed, in question, Ms. Peterson." The man's wild eyes spelled defiance, his voice rang with disbelief, as though opposition were the point here. Indeed, hostility may have been his foremost skill, inexperienced as he was otherwise for his appointment. A pressed suit, bald head, and graying beard lent him the sort of credibility he should have had to earn, a free pass Jennifer wished were hers, at times, gender notwithstanding.

He pushed an incongruous argument. "All the graphs of past advancement show steady progress, not a sharp upturn. They do not predict wildly disparate future trends. At least, not the trends you're talking about. Human thought is not and never wil be a mechanical process." Several of the co-panelists concurred. One after another disparaged her sources.

Jennifer felt that she was losing them again and mentally regrouped. *Money guys aren't science guys*, she reminded herself. "Okay," she said, capitulating. "Let's look at it another way. Say, for the moment, time doesn't exist." Her smartwatch beeped the hour into the microphone, and someone in the audience laughed.

"Okay, maybe it exists"—she chuckled—"but it no longer directs the *pace* of advancement. As my colleagues have predicted, in just a few short years, technological progress will literally run away with time. We must be ready for it." She hoped her practical tone would convey what she considered obvious logic. When no one challenged her, she went on, "Our understanding of the human brain, when applied to genetic engineering and nanoscience at a calculable rate, shows an exponential upturn, which, in turn, will boost itself exponentially. We are just a decade or two from being able to create thinking machines that will outstrip our own capacity in every way." She raised her voice above the mumurs. "Every way *except for one:* the ability to feel."

"You got that right," came a catcall from the dim room.

An uneasy silence gave Jennifer another moment to calm herself.

She continued. "If robots could feel, they could help man build on our greatest strength and overcome our greatest weakness: emotion." She moved away from the podium, playing to the audience now, pacing in time with her words. "Many argue that how we feel makes us human… and yet it clouds our good judgment, even when lives are at stake. This reliance on the heart regarding matters of the mind, I believe, is what holds us back from further evolution."

Silence, and then a stream of angry murmurs.

Jennifer returned to the podium for the stability it offered. Her voice rose. "*Consider, if you will*, not a life without sentiment, but one that masters it and gets the most from its power—like a sailing ship navigating stormy seas." She pulled her phone from a pocket and used it to illustrate her point, projecting an image of buffeting waves toward the audience. "Yes, the captain must calculate—using sexton or stars or GPS." She glanced at the ceiling, and pretended to sail the precarious phone/boat through the air. "But the captain must also intuit—how much force the masts can take, when to raise and lower sails, when to head for the lifeboats, if need be. Using only computation, she fails." The boat prop dipped. "Using only gut sensation, she fails." She upended the boat and let it slowly sink behind the rostrum.

The hall was silent.

Jennifer went on, "The question is, ladies and gentlemen, how can we, as humans, find the place in our future where intellect meets instinct? How can we steer toward the current that will carry us to the next shore?"

A female panelist leaned forward and interjected, "More importantly, Ms. Peterson: why should we put money behind such a theoretical effort?"

Jennifer eyed her, supressing a retort about Christopher Columbus, then addressed the full panel. "We've gone beyond theory already. In reverse-engineering the brain, we have made great strides—measurable, documented strides—in understanding and replicating discrete mental processes: data computation, pattern recognition, even simple problem solving. But the processes that require an element of emotional instinct, or learned emotion—matters of moral and ethical standing, the "gray" areas that extend like an ocean deep within our minds—these are what will propel us to the next stage of our human destiny."

She held her breath, knowing that this outcome was both unpopular and inevitable. A few years earlier, she could have sold it wholesale, but the science hadn't been solid. Now, in the current sociopolitical climate, the body of evidence had itself become a drawback. Facts were suspect. Those who peddled them, more so.

"Our model is simple," she assured the funding board members. She spread her hands. "We conduct a wide-scale, global survey of ethics, running all the data, potential conflicts, and psychological responses through our computers. From this, the machines 'learn'—they extrapolate, with appropriate variables, thousands of times over, millions of times over. What do we do with that information? We average it. We get a consensus. We turn gray into black and white, nuanced by every color in between." She nodded in the direction of her two university colleagues, seated behind her, and took a deep breath. This was it. "We aim to apply technological advancement to human intelligence. To do so, we contend that the mapping of emotion holds the key to creating higher intelligence that employs creative, critical, and compassionate thinking."

For a moment, nobody moved. The claim that should have easily floated seemed to drop like a hammer into a lake.

Then the moderator retorted, his voice thick with derision. "Compassion. And how, may I ask, does one code for that?"

Two women at his end of the dais jostled each other.

Jennifer ignored them. "That is why we are seeking federal support, Dr. Ragenfeld. Our research intends to join intelligence engineering with ethical consensus. We propose—"

"Whose ethics?" the moderator shot back. "Yours?"

One of the more temperate panelists ventured, "Yes, how do we know that this… data, rather than personal opinion, would bring you to this consensus?"

"Well, I—"

"Admit it! You cannot provide this assurance!" Ragenfeld shouted. "This is a blatant ploy to both fund and codify your radical agenda."

"… in the guise of 'controlling' robots that can't be controlled," the panelist next to him put in snidely. "Some lines just shouldn't be crossed."

Corroborating outbursts swelled among the seats.

"We beg to differ." Jennifer's throat tightened. She gripped the podium, and her mind whirled with comebacks, each quickly rejected as too inflammatory. She settled on a line from an old Spaulding Gray film that had stuck with her over the years: "With due respect to the panel, morality is not a movable feast. We start from a point that we can all agree…" This last was drowned out by a no-longer-contained tumult from those listening, both on the stage and in the risers.

As if to show the strength of their numbers, someone threw open the hall doors, and a knot of angry protestors pushed their way in, chanting, "No A.I.! No A.I.! No A.I.!"

"They'll take our jobs!" somebody yelled, and the crowd surged down the ramp toward the stage. Hand-drawn placards bobbed above their heads: HUMAN RIGHTS ARE FOR HUMANS; ARTIFICIAL INTELLIGENCE ISN'T SMART; and YOU CAN'T PROGRAM LOVE. One simply proclaimed, STOP SCIENCE!

Ragenfeld and his cronies appeared more pleased than worried at the flood of marchers, proving the theory, Jennifer thought bitterly, that reptilian thinking *was* the thing holding the human race back from its climb up the evolutionary ladder. She regarded the smug panelists, resignation building. They would make their funding decision based on emotions, which were now running high—and not favorably in her direction. She sighes. Ironic that such a knee-jerk reaction would get in the way of actually doing something about knee-jerk reactions.

"No A.I.! No A.I.!"

Jennifer threw a look over her shoulder at her two lab partners. Their stricken faces told her the threatening wave of fear had broken and was about to come crashing down on them. Never mind the funding, they'd be lucky to escape with their lives. As one, they grabbed their devices full of notes and lurched for the rear exit.

>>> <<<

Jennifer's brain dutifully recalled the tenor of that past moment and signaled her gallbladder to release a measure of fluid, which rose in her throat and brought back the full sensation of that fiasco. She pursed her lips against the taste, and swallowed rather than defile the laboratory floor.

"And *that* was your peak fail?" Jennifer's staff member asked, in a voice that was less robot and more human radio announcer. The machine had been listening with rapt attention.

Jennifer eyed the stylized clown head, a holographic image projected from the dark pebble that housed her mechanical assistant supervisor, Jack16.

"Yes," she answered. "Definitely my biggest fail." She wrinkled her nose against the aftertaste. "Bile to the tenth power. Thanks for asking."

Jack instantly sifted through his database on historic social movements that had opposed scientific advancement. "And this would have occurred sometime during the first portion of the nineteenth century?" he surmised, in all sincerity.

"Luddites? I wish," Jennifer said. In fact, it had happened less than a dozen years before, when she'd been looking for a way to fund her doctoral research. "But it's like Dad always said: failure's just a part of learning. Take skiing, for instance. If you don't fall, you're not learning. You know, what doesn't kill us makes us stronger, and all that." She paused, listening to the CPU buzz as it assimilated this information. "So, tell me, Jack. What was your biggest fail?" She caught herself, fooled momentarily by the machine's realistic dialogue matrix. "Wait. Dumb question."

"No question is 'dumb,'" the robot reminded her. "Only the questioner."

"Right," Jennifer muttered, perplexed. "It's never the program's fault; it's the programmer's." To save face, she added, "Deactivate conversation mode," and Jack fell silent and fluttered into oblivion.

The corners of Jennifer's mouth drifted upward.

>>> <<<

Jennifer thought about the exchange on her way home from the glass studio, and mulled where her path had taken her since the fateful day she'd described. The empty street around her seemed especially hushed in contrast to the chaotic scene in her mind—one which had ended in escape from the shouts and threats of the protestors as the glares of the panelists burned holes in the scientists' backs.

Sure, the episode had been devastating at the time. But it hadn't been the end of the world. Sometimes, Jennifer thought, failing turned out to be a stepping stone to another way of doing things.

She nodded at two pedestrians who passed by, their words muted in the vacant street. Only a few more late-shift denizens prowled Olympic City-3 at this hour, a time when Jennifer often sought solitude in the glassblowing studio to clear her mind and do some serious thinking. She turned to follow a landscaped pedway that spiraled up from the city's lowest level, her determination sitting like an undigested peach pit in her stomach.

She hadn't let the short-sighted panelists and pro-testors stop her from advancing her notion of infusing a manufactured intelligence with a sense of self, and therefore, right and wrong. In the intervening years, her conviction had only grown that this technology was the next logical step in human future. The stubborn idea had first taken hold when she was child, gazing in wonder at the petroglyphs in eastern Montana's stonescapes. These long-ago messages led her to think from where the human race had been to where it one day might go. No skepticism from politicos, or lack of funding, or even sudden affluence could change its course. So she had remained on course.

She'd formed alliances outside the States, finding common cause with researchers in Sweden and Japan who were more than happy to share the survey studies they'd undertaken for other purposes. For the next ten years, she had painstakingly extended their findings via computer models, inching forward, then back, then forward again, always finding a way past the momentary setback. When she fell in deep powder, she'd remind herself, she had no choice but to plant her skis, get back up, and schuss down the mountain… or lie out there and die. So she'd kept at it, finally finding stable ground in the Western Land Core, a consortium of former U.S. states whose government had embraced advancement, not shunned it.

The haunting strains of Mozart's funeral mass replayed in her head as she walked up the ramp, rising higher and higher toward her family's pod level. The puzzle she'd held at the back of her mind in the studio slid forward, and she fussed with it a bit. Perhaps she did have enough raw material to feed into the master program, to see if she were any closer to her to goal. Was she being too careful? Or just avoiding a grand risk?

She frowned. "Now I know where Chris gets it from." Her twelve-year-old son was forever deliberating, rarely deciding for sure. But Jennifer knew better than to take the safe road. Tomorrow she would run a few trials on Val, another computation robot at the lab. It would all be in keeping with the department's usual quotas. No one needed to know. Which would play especially well if things didn't work out.

Jennifer approached her front door, and the large frosted-glass panels sensed her arrival and transitioned into clear glass. She heard the door's *hiss–click,* and a sharp bark greeted her from inside as the entrance parted in front of her.

"Shh, Maxi!" She stepped across the threshold and onto a thick red, green, and black mat that muted the sound of her feet. She glanced at the marble statue of the goddess Minerva in an alcove backlit with a soft, blue glow that dimly illuminating the tiled entryway. George must have left the light on for her when he went to bed.

Two more barks shrilled their way into the quiet foyer before she could reach down and pat the dog to quiet it. At her mistress's touch, the little reddish-brown furball wiggled her bottom fiercely, marching in place, tiny metal claws ticking on the tile. Maxi, a miniature Australian shepherd, had thick synthetic fur and erect ears with tips that flopped down into triangles. Jennifer lingered in a crouch, smiling at her pet, whose two ice-blue eyes locked onto her deep-blue ones and, she was sure, bored directly into her soul.

She straightened up, and another *hiss-click* preceded the emergence of a door down the hallway.

"Jesus, Ma," a voice scolded, and a girl's head popped into the space, roughly at Jennifer's height. Her magenta-colored hair was mussed and her gray eyes sleepy, brow and lips drawn into a scowl. "Do you have to make so much noise in the dead of night?"

"Don't swear, Sabrina," Jennifer said, inwardly chuckling at her daughter's brazenness. This was a child who would clearly outgrow her older brother and her mother in stature before long, and who seemed to have been around the block far more times than her nearly ten years would allow.

"'Jesus' is not a swear. I looked it up."

Jennifer wagged a finger at her. "Context, Brin, honey. It's all in the context."

CHAPTER 2

Had it not been for a cheap pen and the laws of gravity, George and Jennifer might never have met. The petite, blonde woman pointed to the name scrawled on George's notebook and read, "George… Xical, no?" She pronounced the surname correctly—SHE-cal—instantly charming her classmate and drawing his respect. He rose, the pen forgotten in his hand, and stared at her. He had never seen eyes so profoundly lovely in his life.

If George Xical had to pinpoint the instant he'd fallen for his future wife, it would have been that first day in class when he'd retrieved her fallen pen. Jennifer had taken it and met his gaze with her incredible blue eyes, saying, "*Muchas gracias.*" Her use of the Spanish propelled his already ascending heart into the stratosphere so swiftly it broke the sound barrier. In fact, head spinning, he didn't hear her next words, whatever they were.

Jennifer Peterson's unenhanced irises shone, well, iris-blue—a deep cerulean with a violet cast and nearly imperceptible flecks of gold and black, like the flower. They were so striking and meaningful to George that he included their image in his daily meditation, his cure-all for the intensities of life. Whatever the distraction, from a hangnail to the birth of his children or the death of his family members in the war, the daily refresher let George reset his head and heart, and find peace at the end of the day.

Lately, this was more easily said than done. The apportionment secretary's duties for Western Land Core central command had reached a crescendo—but these paled in comparison to his demanding role of stay-at-home dad. Now, as his son, Chris, fired off question after rhetorical question, George restrained his natural urge to answer and, instead, focused on the boy's gray eyes. These were curiously devoid of the Impressionist-inspired iris patterns he'd inherited from his mother. Both Chris and Sabrina had lost their original eye color when they'd received their pediatric security implants, a procedure Jennifer had insisted upon. Set against brown skin a shade or so lighter than George's own and framed by thick, black, shoulder-length hair that turned upward at the ends, Chris's chromium eyes never stopped searching for clues.

"So, how am I supposed to get more sleep?" the gangly preteenager asked. "I've never had less free time. Between homework and guitar lessons and band practice, I'm up later than ever. And does Mom care? She loads on the chores. If it's not babysitting for Brin or manning the soup kitchen, then it's researching service options. Dad. I'm twelve. Do I really have to start worrying about national service now?"

George opened his mouth to answer.

Chris continued, "The answer is no. None of my friends are bothering, and the ones I know who have actually served say it's not a big deal. I mean, do you think it's a big deal?"

George's mouth closed while he pondered this. His and Jennifer's families had proud histories of public service, although enlistment hadn't always been required. This made it more noteworthy, to his mind. George wanted his children to cultivate the same motivation, on their own terms, before the choice became compulsory.

"Of course it's a big deal, but not now," Chris supplied. "I mean, I'm always tired. Do you know what that's like?"

George waited to see if the boy would answer this last one. Chris sat on the corner of his father's black office desk, his face lit by a rippling reflection. The empty slab of obsidian created a virtual interface from which George had been working. His son's overlong arms and leg, thin as bundles of reeds, had already reached their growth limit and would have a few years of waiting for the rest of him to catch up. Though he shared his father's complexion, Chris had his mother's thin, angular eyebrows and lips and quick, expressive hands. His lush black eyelashes matched his hair, and both were so long that many people mistook him for girl—until they noticed his feet, which—like his larger limbs—had achieved maturity, at size thirteen.

"You probably don't remember how hard it is to be twelve." Chris cocked his head at his father. "You were my age, when? Like, a hundred years ago?"

George's inward grimace didn't mar his measured expression. *Enjoy it while you can, kid,* he thought. The boy couldn't know that sleep became a more elusive companion the older one got. In fact, the issues facing the Core right now had all but ensured insomnia, what with the prospect of hostile borders intruding on everything from WLC outreach efforts to the family vacation. A few extra hours' sleep would be a godsend, he thought, tuning his son out and turning over his worries like fresh earth. He was so caught up in the cycle that he didn't hear what Chris was hoping he wouldn't hear.

>>> <<<

"And I'm failing classic lit. I can't help it if that stuff puts me to sleep," the boy said. "When I mentioned it to our counselor, he said I'd be able to stay awake if I got more sleep in the first place. So I told him how busy I am, and he said he needed to talk to you about it on Monday, first thing, but I told him we were going on vacation and would be out of cell range. He said, 'Where're you going, the moon?' and I said, 'Just the U.S.' Which might as well be the moon. So, it'll have to wait. Right?" Chris's cheeks were pink with the effort at sugarcoating the problem for his father.

"Hmm?" George said absently. "Mm-hmm," he agreed, just as removed.

Chris slowly let out a breath, then resumed his commentary to further ease his way past a punishment. Sometimes he could read George like a blog post. That blank gaze was a dead giveaway that his father had left the building. It was as if the man had a third eyelid, like the nictitating membranes of frogs that Chris had correctly identified on the last life science test. His lab partner had rolled her eyes and scoffed at his perfect score, saying studying was a waste of time since, pretty soon, all their thinking would be done for them by computers anyway.

Chris's stomach lurched at the thought. True, he might not have wanted to train his mind on less attractive subjects than frogs, like dusty works of literature that seemed wholly removed from his reality. But figuring out how to do new things was intoxicating. And it was about the only virtual controlled substance a twelve-year-old could get his hands on. Every new guitar riff that seemed to come out of nowhere made Chris crave more, and suggested to him that the next thrill was right around the corner. Mom had even let him blow his own guitar slide in the glass studio when he wished he had one to match his blood-red Fender. That had only taken six or eight tries. He finally formed one that fit over his index finger. What would he do if it were all done for him?

He shuddered.

"What do you think, Dad? When robots get smarter, are we going to get dumber? And will our minds turn to moosh? That's what Jillis says." Apprehension lingered in his voice.

He watched George's brownish-black eyes swim back into focus, straining to recall the last comment that had clearly caused his son some concern. Today Dad's long, black, silver-streaked hair was pulled back in a ponytail, accentuating his symmetrical facial features—the thick, straight eyebrows, high crescent cheekbones, straight nose with its two perfect phalanges, and pillowed lips. Even George's ears were notable in their prominent proportions and refined shape, like two ornamental vases that beckoned sound the way conical blossoms attracted hummingbirds.

"Dad?"

"Don't worry about it, son," George said, his hesitation only amping the volume of Chris's uneasiness.

George's facial expression did not betray his thoughts, but it was his father's hands that Chris kept watch on. When the rest of him was unreadable, George's hands never lied. Right now, they were balled tight, contradicting his words.

"I want to know," Chris pressed, tensing his own fists. "If robots take over our thinking, will we have to give up playing guitar?" He ended on a frantic note.

George's dark eyes trained on his, the third eyelid retracted. "I don't think so. No. Creativity will be the last hurdle for A.I., and it may be a moot point after we integrate. For now, though, researchers haven't been able to jump the gap yet."

Chris tilted his head, sensing that his father was holding something back. "Yeah. But will they?"

George paused. He tried never to mislead his children, but the truth was… complicated. "If they do manage that level of intelligence, Chris, it will be nothing to fear." He reached out and grasped his son's shoulders. The strong, sure fingers, toned from hours on the fretboard, were more relaxed now, and served to verify what he'd said.

Chris sighed once more in relief.

His father rose and touched the back of his ear, activating his intercom. "Sabrina. Help your brother supervise dinner. Your mother will be home in a few minutes." A pause; then George's head recoiled, presumably from the sudden noise in his earpiece.

It was loud. Chris could hear his sister's usual chaotic soundtrack compete with her reply. Talk about immature. Her response was unintelligible, but its nature was clearly read in George's tightened lips and subsequent dash for the door.

Kids, Chris thought, and sauntered after him.

>>> <<<

The day had not been as productive as Jennifer would have liked. She'd spent hours with Val2001, trying to get an independent value judgment out of the robot. Jennifer's hunch that a critical mass of data would be enough to kick-start the computer's powers of deduction in the realm of ethical reasoning remained unconfirmed. But then again, Jennifer told herself, it hadn't been denied, either.

The theory was sound. Based on the body of data in its memory plus its ability to pull an infinite amount of information from the Internet, the robot *should* be able to learn how to learn, and therefore teach itself new things. That it hadn't yet was not evidence to the contrary. Far from discouraging Jennifer, such inconclusiveness got under her skin and itched, not so much an irritant as a stimulus. Perhaps annoyance was the reason she hadn't given up in all these years.

That's why, Mom, she silently answered her mother's perennial question: why do you have to be so stubborn? *If it weren't for bull-headed people like me, robots would still be stuck in science fiction.* Not that the creator of R2D2 and C3PO hadn't been on the right track.

A truly human-level thinking machine needed an ethics component; that was a given in every legitimate scientific circle. But what was it that made people *decide to decide* what was right and just? If Jennifer could isolate that motivation, she'd be able to allow the system to learn from itself. And then, based on the billions of bits of data that she'd spent the past decade compiling and accessing, the technology should be able to make humanlike choices—on its own.

Jennifer had situated herself ideally for this task. She'd taken the job of district Ethics Engineer based in the Olympic Cities, a consolation prize awarded by the Western Land Core brain trust when it mothballed her research program, soon after the last Mexican War. Back then, the newly formed coalition of Western states had to make economic sustainability its top priority, and rightly so, at the time. Whether knowingly or not, the administrators had thrown her the juiciest bone possible, one that would facilitate getting on with her work.

On the surface, she was a manager of managers—the human supervisor for a fleet of computer robots programmed for a plethora of deductive tasks to help run the government and city physical plant. The bots were sufficiently advanced in intelligence to decide which infrastructure and policy measures to implement and how to go about them… to a point. When they reached a crossroads beyond their capacities—such as when faced with questions requiring knowledge of social mores or historical consequences—they relayed the matter to the E.E. Then Jennifer followed admin guidelines to make a recommendation, which was referred to committee, and sometimes even went out to the public for a direct vote.

The results of the thousands of issues she'd handled over ten years eventually became fodder for Val2001's edification. One of thirty-two hundred machines on Jennifer's team, Val appeared to be just an ordinary robot flak churning out the routine assessments that kept the country and city running on a short human staff. But Jennifer had secretly been adding classified ethical-decision data to the technological mind's memory. Someday, she would make Val the prototype for pure artificial consciousness on a level that would equal and surpass that of humans in every way. Researchers had already been able to replicate most of these cognitive abilities—with the major exception of the dead zone that was ethical thinking. Jennifer was betting on the theory of data saturation to provide the missing link.

At least, until today. She'd come up with a sample question: *What amount of economic subsidy will significantly improve an individual's standard of living without eliminating the motivation to contribute to society?* The test would perform double duty, since it bore on the topic of wealth distribution, George's current main mission. He could thank her for solving that one, along with moving the entire human race closer to reaching its full potential. Jennifer fed Val the question.

Val had kicked it out and referred it back to management. Damn.

It might be that the saturation point was farther off than Jennifer had calculated. Or it could be that her theory was missing a vital step.

In any case, her work with Val had gone far enough that she wasn't comfortable leaving her files on the machine's hard drive. Anyone with lab clearance could inadvertently download or scrub them—or they could be hacked, she supposed, by a hostile interest. Although, nobody else but George and Mena knew about them. In any case, she wasn't taking chances that they'd be stolen. Carrying such information around on a thumb drive was out of the question.

So, at the end of her session, she transferred the files via a quantum-encrypted wireless link directly from Val2001 to Maxi, her pet, who always accompanied her to work. The dog's operating system included generous memory storage. There'd be no record and nothing to raise suspicion. Then Jennifer whistled, and Maxi followed her out of the building.

>>> <<<

A half-hour after Jennifer got home from work, Sabrina sat in her bedroom before a tray of food, picking the shrimp off her pizza. Why wasn't there an app for this? Talk about consequences.

All she'd done was go up to the rooftop observatory to catch the sunset before dinner, and all hell had broken loose in Parentland. Yes, she'd left after her father had ordered her and Chris to the kitchen. Yes, they'd had to GPS her and come get her, since she'd left her wireless intercom glasses downstairs. But it wasn't Sabrina's fault that her parents were living in the Dark Ages and wouldn't let her get smart contacts. Who did Dad think he was, the president of the United States?

Now she was trapped in her orange-carpeted bedroom, door locked and music privileges revoked.

They can't tell me what to do 24/7, she groused to herself, lips pursed against the hated shrimp that she shunned in a pile on the plate. *And they can't tell me what to like.*

Or not like. *Shrimp, gahh.* She had gone salmon fishing once when she was little and Grandpa Rip had visited, and they'd used live shrimp for bait. The "sea bugs," as she'd termed them, had awaited their execution in a metal pail covered with a paper bag. While Rip fiddled with the fishing gear, Sabrina peeked inside the bait bucket. To her horror, the shrimp spoke to her. Their pops and squeaks plainly called, "Get us out of here!"

When Sabrina relayed this message to her grandfather, though, Rip paid her no mind. "Shrimp don't talk," he'd said, deliberately skewering one on a hook as big as his thumb and forefinger.

"But they do, Grandpa. They are!" Sabrina ripped the bag off the pail and let the brown paper tumble down the pier in the breeze.

Rip calmly drew his arm back and cast his hook-and-bait package into the Puget Sound. "You're imagining too much," he said. "Any noises they make are too low for humans to hear."

But Sabrina knew her ears hadn't deceived her. How could they? Her head sported two elephantine vessels on either side, the auditory legacies of her father's Aztec ancestry. She couldn't unhear the cry for help, and she would never, ever, she vowed, eat a shrimp.

This logic hadn't trickled down to *moo*s and beef or *baa*s and lamb, but there was no accounting for taste, Sabrina thought, glowering down at her plate. Of course, if she'd gone into the kitchen to supervise the dinner robot as her father had directed, she wouldn't be left with a cheese and seaweed pizza and a mound of unwanted sea bugs.

Sushi pizza. *Dad's revenge*, she thought.

Her father was a proud man, and Sabrina was unaware that she shared that trait—a self-esteem so fiercely held that it was evident in their bearing. At just ten years of age, her sturdy posture, broad shoulders, and decisive gait echoed George's. Perhaps this demeanor threatened other children; it would explain Sabrina's difficulty in blending into her school's blended-age groups. Her friends were the ones who were looking for a leader or who were left out of the other cliques. Young Sabrina Peterson was definitely happiest when she was in charge. This she got from her mother.

A knock came at the bedroom door, which swished open to reveal her maternal parent. Jennifer eyed the untouched plate and sullen diner, then took a seat next to her daughter on the bed. She set a green drink on the small table. "I thought you might need some more nutrition," she said in a slightly conciliatory tone.

Sabrina tensed. This meant she'd have to give up something in return.

"Isn't it against the law to lock kids in their rooms?" she said coldly. "What if I had to go to the bathroom? What if there was a fire?"

"What if there was a fire in the bathroom?" Jennifer joked mildly, then grew more serious. "You know the rules about wearing your smartglasses, young lady. There are reasons, and there are consequences."

"Like forcing someone to eat something gross?" Sabrina picked up a shrimp and threw it back down on the pile.

"Nobody's forcing you."

"I can't even go upstairs to watch the sunset if I want?"

Jennifer sighed. "Brin. You need to learn to manage your time. It's something you'll have to do as an adult, so get used to it."

Manage this, manage that. It was all her mother seemed to do. Sabrina said nothing.

"Your father is wondering whether you want to take this trip or stay home. If you want to go, you'll have to apologize."

Sabrina was torn. Of course, she wanted to go on vacation. But somewhere exciting, not boring, old Montana, where her tedious cousins played with filthy animals and there was no Internet.

"Could I stay at Mena's instead?" Her mother's best friend, Philomena Fine, lived in the newest canal city, and she let Jennifer's kids have the run of the place.

"Not an option. She's in the middle of a court case. You'd have to stay here with a babysitter."

"Figures." The trip would mean hours and hours of riding in an old-fashioned car, and then days and days away from her social network.

"Don't you want to see Mik and Liz?" Jennifer cajoled. "I hear they've got some new baby chicks. And you've got a newborn cousin you haven't seen yet. Remember?"

Rather than answer, Sabrina invoked her right to pout.

Then the family dog padded silently into the room across the soft, orange flooring that featured a pink swirl, a path that coiled inward to the room's center point.

Sabrina engaged the dog. "Maxi: twirl!" And Maxi spun in circles, following the spiral to its end. Then she plopped down, looking up at her young mistress, light-blue eyes burning like fire on ice. "Good girl." Sabrina tossed her a couple of shrimp, which she caught and ground up for garbage disposal.

"So, we agree you should stick to the schedule," Jennifer persisted. "Will you tell your father you're sorry?"

Sabrina dropped her head in defeat and eyed her mother from behind the shelf of hot-pink hair. She nodded, ever so slightly.

"Okay, then." Jennifer rose and made to leave. So did Maxi.

"Mom? Are we taking Maxi to Harmony?" Sabrina asked, referring to her mother's hometown. That would provide some entertainment. At least the robotic dog was programmed to do awesome tricks. She also didn't drool, stink, or have fleas.

"You bet." Jennifer nodded. "I wouldn't let her out of my sight."

CHAPTER 3

"Absolutely unacceptable," George barked into the microphone. "It's not complete. I won't say it is."

"But it's nearly done, and right on schedule."

The video on the wall screen showed the speaker to be a slender man, younger than George, with no gray in his bushy black hair and an expression of false camaraderie on his brown face. He wore the same blue and green WLC jersey that George usually wore, when he wasn't traveling internationally. Today George felt somewhat out of place and overly casual on the official call, in a black silk T-shirt and indigo jeans.

The caller continued, "All we need is an on-air statement. Jenkins wants the public to see 'City Access' as a win, now."

"You mean, she wants Grubb to see our people getting ahead while his fall behind." The public-housing project they were discussing represented a high-profile contrast to the neighbor country's shredded social safety net. As climate change drove residents away from desert and oceanfront areas, the new smartcities would be ready to receive them. "Don't get me wrong," George put in. "This is a clear success story, by any standards. It brings us one step closer to leveling the playing field. I'm all for that—once we do what we set out to do. But I won't play to the cameras, Sandeep."

"Stop being such an ass, Xical. We need this one."

"Then let's be grown-ups and celebrate work when it's complete, Mr. Ainslee, and not before." This silenced the man for a moment, and George rose to end the meeting. "As you can see, I'm on my way out of town for the holiday. Before I go, though, I'll instruct my office to give no comment on the subject. You'll have to find someone else… although I strongly advise that you don't. This administration needs scrupulous honesty and transparency in order to keep the public trust, especially with all the propaganda to the contrary coming from the U.S."

"Ameristates," Ainslee corrected him. "The trademark changed three years ago. Keep up."

George scowled. "Names change; history doesn't. And our government still won't recognize that stolen mess of a regime." He closed his notebook and tucked it under his arm. "A few more weeks won't diminish the project's success—in the eyes of our public or theirs. I stand by the contract date. Now, I must be off."

"What should I tell Jenkins, then?" The question was loaded with threatened consequences.

"Tell her whatever you like," George growled, and then clicked off. "Infant," he added, weary of trying to respect this mouthpiece for the Core's secretary-general. He suspected Sandeep Ainslee of putting at least an extra turn or two of unnecessary spin on anything coming from the SG's office, probably for his own gain down the road, or so the little twerp thought. Through George's wide-angle lens, whatever benefitted the most people benefitted each person most.

In this view, he and his wife were seamlessly aligned. In getting packed and out of the house, however, they were not.

"Biometric passport?" Jennifer called to George as he left his office and met the entire family in the hallway, scrambling to get packed. Maxi, the dog, paced excitedly between them.

The deliberate shift from work mode to dad-going-on-vacation mode did not occur quickly enough for Jennifer, it seemed.

"Passports?" she repeated impatiently.

George hesitated. "Uh, woops. Didn't download 'em yet."

His wife swept past him. "I'll grab them; you stick the bags in the garage elevator."

George stopped in the hallway. "Er, bags?"

"They're right in front of you, hon'—except for yours," she tossed over her shoulder and slipped into his office.

"Mine? Can you get it?"

"I didn't see yours! Use your phone to find it!" Jennifer yelled from the office.

That was because he hadn't packed it. This housing complex thing had consumed his attention all week. So he'd never packed, and never synced the suitcase to his phone. He set off for the bedroom and then stopped short again. "*¡Caramba!*" he mouthed. Had he charged the vehicle last night?

"Don't swear, Dad," Sabrina scolded.

George looked down at his feet, where Sabrina crouched, attempting to stuff one more pair of shoes into a bag that already wouldn't close. Maxi barked at her.

"It's not swearing just because it's Spanish," he grumbled.

"*¡Caramba!*" Chris said as he knocked his sister with the duffle he was leading down the corridor.

"Dad!"

"I'm not cursing," Chris smugly informed her. "It's like saying, *Gee, whillickers* and *golly darn gosh.*"

"Then I can say it all I want," she retorted, raising her voice. "Get your *caramba* butt down to the *caramba* car, *caramba hermano.*"

Maxi began hopping up and down on her pneumatic legs, giving sharp *yip*s.

This was already more activity than George wanted on a Saturday morning. "Enough! You two set your stuff by the garage elevator. I'll go get the rest and meet you at the car."

Fortunately, Jennifer had plugged in the car on her way home the night before. They would miss its self-driving function, which was allowed only in the largest Canadian metro areas and still outlawed in the States. Twenty minutes later, they pulled the vehicle into the red diamond lane used for manual operation and headed north out of OC-3, bound for Canada.

A welcome silence reigned as George's family took advantage of the Internet connection that would be lost the next day, when they left Alberta for whatever it was they were calling Idaho and Montana that week—the two states had merged when bankruptcy threatened. Sponsorship of the American states rose and fell with the stock market, as the death of one corporation heaped good fortune on the next. And the Xicals and Petersons would subsidize it by paying the hefty duty fee required of visitors entering through a third country, the only safe way to go.

How much longer will this tightrope hold? George wondered. Before the Western split, when the coastal states had contemplated breaking away from the U.S., no one dreamed that travel or trade between the two would be restricted; both sides needed them too much. But the president was big on grudges and light on diplomacy. His team had only to look at their nation's past relations with Cuba to devise a grating policy that would punish former citizens for daring to leave their homeland—and to cash in on tourists.

Still, it was hard for George to get used to. As Ainslee had reminded him, it had been a few years since the new cruelty was implemented: armed guards outside WLC borders, travel directed through a third country, and reentry accompanied by the fees and interrogations that would never seem commonplace to someone who had grown up in a free country. How much longer even those accommodations would last was anyone's guess.

George forced himself to pay attention as he maneuvered the navy-blue family sedan along the interior freeway. His kids would probably never learn to drive, now that autonomous vehicles were the norm—at least, on their side of the divide. The lush landscape seemed to fly past; hydroponic planters filled with flowering bougainvillea enlivened the underground commuter route that circled the city. George knew the layout so well, he could see the rest of OC-3 in his head. Next level up was the city basement, the working sector that held warehouses and workshops, like Jennifer's glassblowing studio, also cheerily landscaped and artificially lit to reflect the outdoors's natural arc of daylight. Next level, the ground floor, which spread out like spokes from a central hub of greenspace, with the watery reaches of Puget Sound and the old brick-and-mortar downtown beyond. One day, when Old Seattle lay underwater, only the smartcities would remain.

Designed to rise with the seas and provide a controlled environment, these enclaves had popped up all along the Pacific Coast during the past ten years. Those meant to supersede Seattle clustered around the spot where the Olympic Mountains spilled into Puget Sound. Among fifteen floating islands, the one George and his family called home held dozens of residential and commercial buildings that housed the city's 213,653 souls, all connected by pedways and mixed-use paths. Architecturally speaking, it was all up from there.

The sedan shot out of the underground, past the massive virtual scaffolding and robotic cranes of the new pods constructing themselves at the edge of the waterborne city. It was all George could do to not focus on their progress. *Drive*, he commanded himself.

The tower assembly had caught Jennifer's eye, too, and she admired the residences. "Wow, they're going up fast.".

"Right on schedule," George remarked.

Jennifer heard the note of bitterness in his voice. "Problem with that?"

"SG's office has one; I don't."

He explained the argument he'd had with Ainslee that morning. The ambitious project, nearly completed, would provide new public housing in every smart city in the Core. Secretary-General Jenkins had wanted to tie the ribbon-cuttings to the Peace Week independence holiday, for the extra good press. George, however, knew they couldn't rush the job. After all, it had been calculated to perfection.

Jennifer knew how grating it could be to have someone mess with a well-formed plan. "I'm glad you stuck to your guns," she said. "Just moving people in from the exterior will do more for P.R. than any holiday photo op."

"I suspect that Barb Jenkins wants to rub Grubb's nose in it. I wish she'd drop the rivalry and just let us get on with our work."

Jennifer gave him a long look. "Nobody said building a new country would be easy." She half-turned to get a second look at the construction they were leaving behind. "I guess it'll take us another generation to get past this childish in-fighting shit and truly unify."

George glanced in the rearview mirror. Both children in the backseat gave no notice to their mother's use of the vernacular. He returned his attention to the highway signs and navigated the ramp to the interstate.

As they drove on, the freeway edged in and out of view of the smartcities that adorned the coastline, many of them still under construction. Jennifer called the kids' attention to a few designed to showcase their themes. "Look, guys!" She waved at cluster of buildings shaped like sailboats and flying colorful flags—a marina community that promised a boat in every driveway—and another settlement featuring the facade of a Roman fortress. This prompted fanciful talk of constructing their own islands, Jennifer's made entirely of glass, and Chris's a Wild West village.

"If I could live anywhere," Sabrina daydreamed, "it would be all candy, all the time. Marshmallow Island. You could only get there by banana-split boat."

"What about you, Dad?" Chris pestered.

"I am more practical than all of you," George said. "My town is fully climate-controlled and sunny all the time: Las Pieles."

Jennifer raised her eyebrows. "The... Skins?"

George tucked up one side of his mouth. "*Sí*. City of suntans. And nobody wears any clothes."

This drew howls from the backseat and melted the miles away. Soon the car was slowing, and then inching through the line of traffic at the border inspection checkpoint.

Jennifer fished out the file drive that held their passport information, and George plugged it into the computer at the booth. The screen showed a uniformed human male, pleasant yet official looking, speaking to them from some nearby office.

"Welcome to Canada, folks. One moment while I access your files." This actually took several moments. Then came the routine questions. "Purpose of your trip?"

"Passing through to—Ameristates," George recited clumsily.

"Visiting family," Jennifer added.

"Will you be stopping in Canada?"

George gave them the location of their hotel in Lethbridge, about two-thirds of the way into their twenty-hour trip to eastern Montana.

This seemed to satisfy the inspector. "Enjoy your stopover," he said, and raised the automatic gate for them.

They drove through and got out of the car to stretch. George was already stiff.

"Must be getting old," he said and asked Jennifer to switch seats with him and drive. He took possession of Maxi, and when the dog curled up on his lap, George quickly dozed off.

>>> <<<

Jennifer was driving again the next morning, about seven o'clock, when they approached the spot where the national parks overlapped the international border. The car interior was quiet as the passengers absorbed the rugged mountain scenery, dark peaks rising above thick stands of fir and spruce that surrounded the roadway. The conifers' waving green tips broke up the late-summer brown of the underbrush and fanned cool breezes down from the heights.

Usually a nuisance, the five hours tacked onto the trip by the forced roundabout route had been welcome this time. As much as Jennifer longed to see her family back on the farm, the reality of life in the Lower 42—or however many states were left now—always came as a shock. The distinction between the WLC, or even Canada, and today's Ameristates had grown more obvious with each visit. The previous year, they'd found the park closed on the States' side and learned that the federal land had been sold to private developers. Now Jennifer's forearms tensed and her hands tightened on the steering wheel, a sense of dread mounting over what she'd witness this time around.

As the family sedan rolled past the tended shrubbery and THANKS FOR VISITING CANADA! sign at the border, the southbound travelers were greeted by a corridor of shot rock topped with barbed wire. It lined the two-lane road, which lay ominously quiet. Jennifer saw just a truck or two coming the other way, and no traffic in front of them. If the States were trying to discourage tourism, it was working.

She slowed the car as a booth plastered with warning signs came into view, and her stomach clutched with fear. Jennifer had never mentioned it to her parents, but these crossings had become increasingly difficult to endure. What would their reception be this time? If they lucked out and got an old-school government employee who just wanted to cover his ass, they might get off with a delay and some slight humiliation. If it were handled by one of the president's more stringent "company men," well... Jennifer didn't want to consider the outcome.

A lone guard standing in front of its battered metal sliding gate waved Jennifer over to the turnout lane and motioned for the passengers to exit.

Jennifer groaned. "Great. Full inspection."

George urged Sabrina and Chris out of the car. They huddled together with Jennifer and Maxi while the guard plugged their passport files into an electronic notepad that had seen better days. Unsatisfied with the information there, he shot questions at George, ignoring Jennifer, the driver, and typed his answers into the keypad.

The white man's hair and beard were unkempt. He wore a brown uniform that said AMERISTATES in red lettering, above a darker brown patch of fabric from which a former logo had been removed. A lit cigarette—when was the last time Jennifer had seen one of those?—danced precariously between his lips as he posed his questions. Smoke and suspicion hung in the air.

"Nature of your visit?"

The long drive and the man's adversarial tenor wore on George. He cocked his head at his wife. "Why don't you ask her? We're visiting her family."

The guard's lips gripped the cigarette more tightly, and he checked their e-papers. "Government workers, eh? Different last names. Peterson and… EX-i-cal?"

"SHE-cal," Jennifer pronounced for him.

"You two married?" When she affirmed this, he tilted his head at her and admonished, "Most ladies change their names." He paused. "Destination?"

"Harmony," Jennifer answered.

The man typed, then continued, "Religious affiliation?"

Jennifer glanced at George and noticed a flush creep up his neck. "None—not affiliated," she said quickly.

The man eyed her. "Answer the question."

"That *was* her answer," George put in tersely.

"Well... Mom and Dad are Christian," Jennifer said weakly.

"And this animal?"

Before anyone could stop her, Sabrina piped up, "Maxi's never even been to church."

Chris let out an overloud laugh and was shushed by his mother. Maxi correctly interpreted the tension in the air and sat at attention next to Jennifer.

"I mean, quarantine papers!" the guard clarified angrily, once more addressing George, who just stared at him for a moment.

"Quaran—the dog's a damn robot!" George's patience had evaporated.

An icy sweat broke on Jennifer's skin, and she felt a drop roll down her back. What if they confiscated the dog? What if they turned George away as a state enemy?

But, after asking about their country allegiance, the worker double-checked their passports and demanded a payment card. A perfunctory search through the vehicle produced more ill will than contraband, so the guard finally released them. They got back in the car and passed through the lumbering electronic gate, which seemed to shut more swiftly than it had opened, as though to repel nonexistent hordes of infiltrators. SMILE – YOU'RE ON CAMERA, read the welcome notice, right next to a fallen signpost that said, ENTER NG MCCONE COUNTY.

"Holy crap," Jennifer said. She drove a ways and pulled over to let George take the wheel. As she settled into the passenger seat with Maxi, the imagined phantasmagoria of holding cells, custody trials, and firing squads slowly faded. "There's no place like home," she murmured.

CHAPTER 4

It all looked so familiar, in a past-tense sort of way. By early afternoon they crept toward Harmony on the two-lane highway, the car swerving this way and that as George sought to avoid potholes in the cracked asphalt. There was little company on the road, and the vehicles that they did see were all older than the one they were driving. The road widened to four lanes downtown, where every other storefront was vacant or littered with debris. A horse and cart passed them coming the other way when they paused at the flashing, four-way stop sign that had replaced the traffic light. The driver waved.

They sped up again. On the way out of town, Jennifer saw that the grain mill's water tower had come down, the cylindrical reservoir lying on its side, leaving a skeleton of rusty steel legs poking at the sky. George almost missed the turnoff to the farm road. He yanked the wheel to the right at the last moment and nearly hit the carcass of a mule deer that lay by the side of the road.

"Whoa!" Chris exclaimed, whirling in his seat to get another look at the grotesque sight.

"Nearly killed it twice," Sabrina quipped.

Another right-hand turn, and the car bumped down a dirt road whose gravel topping had long since sprayed off into the weeds. A tall timber frame straddled the long, dusty driveway on the right, marking the Peterson property. Upturned horseshoes, agate chunks, and pieces of glass and metal adorned the posts in artful designs.

"There they are!" Jennifer announced.

They pulled into the farm compound, its residents alerted to their arrival by whomever had spotted their dust cloud sweeping across the flat checkerboard of grasslands and bare earth that surrounded the town of Harmony. The family's aged Golden/Labrador mix, Banjo, woofed at them but hung back near the house.

Before she was out of the car, Jennifer's big brother caught her in a headlock of a hug through the open door. When he let go, she smiled up into his broad, clean-shaven, sunburnt face. His mouth and brow had that clenched look that others found off-putting, but which she recognized as signs of willful self-control. Any change in his routine unsettled him to some degree. Uncombed blond hair fell in his hooded eyes, which were the deep violet-blue of Jennifer's without the flecks. "Grant. It's good to see you."

"Jens." He gave her a rundown of the day's schedule, seemingly all in one breath, and she promised to help him feed the animals that evening.

Jennifer synced the bracelet she wore to Maxi's electronic collar, so the dog wouldn't leave her side, and let her out of the car. This brought Banjo up for a sniff, which

Maxi returned; but absent any dog scent from the canine robot, Banjo immediately lost interest and wandered off.

Her parents, Ruby and Rip, had descended on the children, and George had popped the trunk and was rummaging in there for something. He pulled out a fabric shopping bag and handed it to Rip, followed with a handshake. "For your fly-tying," he explained.

Jennifer's father, a vision of Grant with a few decades more of sun exposure etched into his face, thanked George and turned to Jennifer with a stiff hug. "Daughter. I hate to rush you-all, but best hook up your charger in case the electric goes down for the night."

"Never know," her mother added. Ruby Peterson, though slight of build and worn in complexion, conveyed the type of strength that came from a lifetime of managing a farm and family. Her long, loose gray hair, tanned skin, and violet eyes had clearly been softened by close association with nature.

Jennifer hit a button on her bracelet and said to George, "Hon, will you hook Maxi up too? She might need a charge."

While George pulled the sedan next to the dusty carport and hooked it to the outlet, Jennifer went to meet her younger sister, Sheila—who carried a baby in one arm and led one of her two older children by the hand.

"Everybody's home today?" Jennifer asked her mother.

"Not much else but work to do…." she said, letting Sheila in between them to peck her sister on the cheek. The young woman was about five feet tall, the same height as Jennifer but stouter, as she'd never shed all of the added pregnancy weight after each childbirth. Her brownish-blonde hair was pulled back in a pony tail and pinned tightly to her head with a half-dozen plastic clips.

"Dora, isn't it? Hey, little one...." Jennifer fawned over the baby, who had been born eight months before, in between the September family rendezvouses.

Sheila's seven-year-old girl, plump in too-tight pink shorts and a T-shirt, jumped up and down. "I *love* your hair, 'Brina. And your red doggy." She patted Maxi and then smacked Jennifer's cheek when she leaned down for a kiss. "Come see the chicks!" she urged her cousins.

Sabrina and Chris took up with her and ran off to the hen house. Jennifer knew the novelty would wear off quickly, though. The vacation always lasted just long enough for the word *bored* to become Sabrina's mantra.

"Lizzie!" Sheila bellowed after the girl. "Find your brother and send him up to the house."

Jennifer gave her sister a hug and the baby's tiny hand a squeeze, and said, "I'm so happy for you!"

"I am too," Sheila said wryly, "now that Ron's out of the picture." Ron Jones was the latest of Sheila's three husbands. Her hot-and-cold-running relationships had defined her adult life, and colored what might have been the empty-nest years of her parents. But Grant, now thirty-nine, had never left home either. Had Jennifer not gone away to college, the full nuclear family might still be centered here on the outskirts of Harmony, Montana. Ron, however, had taken a powder after some inconsequential argument, relieving the homestead of his presence, at least.

When George reappeared, carrying some things from the car, the group drifted toward the main farmhouse to visit. As they crossed the ramshackle yard where a few wildflowers struggled up through the cracked dirt, Jennifer caught a whiff of something acrid in the air. She scanned the windbreak of spruce trees that ringed the yard and spotted a fuzzy line of black smoke rising behind them.

"Dad!" she caught Rip's elbow and pointed him toward the spot.

"What th'—?"

They all stared. Sheila, standing there with the baby, seemed to know more than the rest of them. "Mikhail Roderick Peterson," she invoked, under her breath. Her eyes clouded over. "I'll kill that boy."

>>> <<<

Mik Peterson took his entertainment where he could find it. The rural areas that had carried President Grubb to victory had been rewarded with the chance to build character by doing more with less. So, opportunities for recreation had grown scarce, the scarcer money and gasoline had become. A guy could only torture cats for so long. *Thank god for cousins,* Mik thought wickedly.

Sabrina and Chris were too young to take seriously and too naive not to mess with. What could he do? City kids were always scared of stuff like coyotes and gunshots and... fire.

Mik poked around the carport for something flammable and came up with a few items. He needed some tinder. Noticing a couple of plywood wheel chocks under the tires of Aunt Jen's dark-blue car, he kicked them aside and added them to his armload. The vehicle was parked at the top of an incline just outside the carport, hooked up to the electrical outlet. Mik looked inside. "Sheesh," he said, spying an inert Maxi lying on the dashboard charger. "Who'd want a robot dog?" At the word *dog*, Maxi opened one eye. But Mik had already turned away. "If *I* had a robot," he went on, "it'd be like the Swiss Army knife of robots. Warrior, computer, slave."

He mused over the fun he could have with that as he carried his supplies down the slope to the burn bin, which was half full of trash. Grandpa probably wouldn't torch it until it was full and the air wasn't so dry, but who would stop Mik now? He could hear Lizzie squawking at their cousins from the chicken yard, and the others were holed up in the house.

Mik squirted some kerosene from a plastic jug into the refuse piled in the rusty fifty-five–gallon barrel, lit a match, and dropped it in. Soon, a nice flower of orange blossomed across the top of garbage. Nice—but not enough to get anybody's attention. He climbed the hill to the carport and brought the leaf blower back with him.

Sure enough, the sound of blower and the resulting shoots of flame attracted his sister and cousins.

Lizzie ran up, frowning. "Mom said she wants you in the house, Mikkie."

"I'm right near the house," he said, tilting his head at the carport. He set down the blower and stepped back a few paces.

"Hey, Mik," Chris greeted him. "Thanks for the warm welcome."

Sabrina joined them. "Fireworks! I love fireworks."

This wasn't going as Mik had envisioned.

"Do ya now?" He picked up a long stick and stirred the trash. Then he reached down for one of the items at his feet. "Want to hear something loud?"

The expression on Chris's face told Mik he didn't. Stupid nodding Sabrina, though, thought she did.

Mik tossed the half-package of old firecrackers he'd found into the barrel. The musty flash powder gave four... six... eight weak reports.

Stupid Sabrina clapped her hands and exclaimed, "Wow! Cool!"

Chris remained unimpressed.

Mik reached for one of the cans at his feet. "That was just a preview." He tossed an aerosol shaving cream can on the pile. "You might wanna stand back."

Lizzie glared at him. "You're not 'posed ta do that!" She ran for the house, up the slope. Outside the carport, she turned an ankle and fell against the charging sedan, earning a *yip!* from the resting Maxi. The child righted herself and kept going.

Chris folded his arms and stared at the fire. "What?"

Mik nodded knowingly. "Sometimes it takes a while." For good measure, he added two more cans.

He saw he had Sabrina's rapt attention. There was nothing like creating a little suspense. The sound of crackling fire and the ugly black smoke rising from the burning garbage added to the effect. As a surge of heat emanated from the mass, Chris nervously backed away a few steps.

Mik stood his ground. He grinned at Sabrina, whose face had gone white. "Don't worry, cuz. They're only little homemade bombs."

Sabrina, though, was goggling beyond him, past the burning spectacle, toward the hillside. "Guys! The—car. It's—"

She'll forget all about the frickin' car in a minute....

But a commotion made Chris swing his head around, and Sabrina yelped and pointed. Mik tried to ignore them. All of a sudden something big slid down the hill his way. Mik froze. Had the damn dog started the car?

Chris dove in one direction and Sabrina in the other. Mik, slower to react, was pushed out of the way—by the bumper of the rolling sedan.

"Aaugh!" The damn thing had rammed his leg. Shouldn't have burnt the chocks.

All three children tumbled roughly to the ground as the wayward car struck the burn barrel. *Toom!* A sharp explosion ripped through the air.

Toom! Toom! The first blast triggered two more, followed by cries of surprise and pain.

Some of the screams were Mik's.

"C'mon!" He scrambled to get away from the car, before it caught fire. His cousins, freaked out and crying, half-crawled and half-stumbled after him. Before he knew how badly anyone was hurt, he hazily wondered, would they hate him for this? Maybe. But, hey: small price to pay.

>>> <<<

Jennifer led the rush through the front yard and carport, and down to a patch of scorched earth where her children and Sheila's boy, Mik, lay on the ground, rocking in agony. Rip headed for the kids, while Grant ran for the hose. The source of the blaze—a trash burn pile—was still on fire. And, inexplicably, their car sat right next to it!

With no thought for her safety, Jennifer hurled herself at the sedan, yanked the door open, and grabbed Maxi.

George reached her. "Go! Let me try to move it!" Without a gas tank, the risk was not as high as it might have been. He got the car started and pulled it past the group, not back up the slight incline that had enabled its escape.

Jennifer, shaking, watched her father assess the children. "Dad?"

"They're—okay. Your mother's calling for help."

Jennifer saw the fuel can and leaf blower used for ignition, still lying there. She crept up and retrieved them, dumping them out in the open, as Lizzie hustled up from the house, followed by Sheila and the baby, who had fallen behind.

"Mikkie!" wailed little Liz, and Jennifer put an arm out to keep her back. Ruby jogged up, and Sheila handed her the baby. Then she, Jennifer, and George looked the kids over.

"Aerosol cans must've blown," Rip informed everyone.

Chris and Sabrina, who had dove away from the moving car, were more frightened than anything else, although they were both sobbing and Sabrina held her hands over her ears. Mik, however, had been hit by a fireball and metal shrapnel as the barrel burst. He groaned, then panted, "I was watching it, Grandpa. I swear. I was just watching it."

"Now, boy," Rip soothed him. "Wadn't your fault."

Jennifer wasn't so sure. She warily eyed her sister's fourteen-year-old boy, his maturing legs sticking out of trouser cut-offs and a red-and-white farmer's tan outlined on his less-developed naked torso, which was bathed in sweat and soot.

"He's burnt some hair and skin off," Rip called over his shoulder. "But it doesn't look worse than second-degree. Do you have some burn cream?" he asked Sheila, helping Mik get to his feet. The boy pressed a hand to his reddened scalp.

"You two, come with me," Sheila ordered, taking Lizzie's hand and leading her son by the elbow, off toward their cottage.

"I was just watching it," Mik repeated, shell-shocked, as they walked off.

Sabrina and Chris sidled up to their mother, who motioned for them to follow her, out of danger. Jennifer expected to hear sirens approach, then remembered that the volunteer fire department had closed and the county hospital hadn't had ambulance service in quite some time.

Ruby's telephone calls had roused a handful of neighbors, though, who converged on the farm with buckets and shovels. By the time they got there, Rip and Grant were wetting down the hay barn siding with hoses, as a precaution.

The group assessed the situation, then set down their fire tools.

"Best let it run its course," suggested one of the neighbor men.

"D'you think it'll spread?" George worried aloud, approaching Jennifer and the kids and drawing them close.

"Naw," the fellow said. "Long as the wind don't come up."

Jennifer broke away and took in the scene, hands gripping her elbows and Maxi at her heels. Burn season was open, but conditions were not ideal. This was the sort of calculation her father had taught her to make as a child. He would never have lit the tinder pile in this type of dry weather. Poor Mik, the product of Sheila's first marriage, was old enough to know better—but young enough or brash enough not to care. Now that she knew Chris and Sabrina were unharmed, she quivered with alarm at how close she had come to losing Maxi and her files.

George mistook her silence for the wrong concern. "Mik'll be alright. If there's real damage, they'll take him to the E.R."

"At least the horses were all out," Jennifer said shakily, nodding at the black dots across a nearby pasture and suddenly feeling guilty for worrying over her computer files. *Why didn't I just leave them at the lab?* she browbeat herself. Now reasonably sure they wouldn't have to evacuate, she left the others and returned to the car for Maxi's carrying case. It felt a bit like closing the barn door after the horses had run off, but Jennifer deactivated her pet and put her inside the case, for safekeeping.

CHAPTER 5

No one had expected such chaos today. The hot summer days around Harmony typically plodded at the pace of outdoor chores. Jennifer could recall as a child fervently wishing for some excitement, or just an unexpected visitor to break up those seemingly endless afternoons, in between feedings, when she had tired even of her books or computer games. Runaway wildfire and traumatic injury had not, however, been on her list.

Ruby brought the neighbors some cold sodas and paid them for the gas they'd used to get there. After they were on their way and Chris and Sabrina were sent to a guest room, the rest of the family congregated in the front room of the farmhouse.

Jennifer's parents had set the manufactured home on the property sometime after Sheila's first marriage, when they'd turned over the original three-bedroom cottage to her. Grant lived in his own trailer at the back of the compound, nearest the stable. The newer home had a modern, four-bedroom layout, with an open kitchen and dining room and a sunken living area beneath a vaulted ceiling.

An electric fan hung from it, arms spinning lazily. The fake logs of an electric fireplace lay dormant beneath a mass-produced wood mantel.

Hardwood floors and a nondescript tan area rug graced the front room, and overstuffed modular seating in a brown-and-orange plaid fabric dominated the space. Piles of belongings—a bundle of knitting, stacks of worn agricultural journals, an empty baby bottle—revealed who sat where. Several alcove shelves were stuffed with Ruby's collection of chicken figurines and Grant's displays of polished rocks. The television set, an old, pre-projection model, sat dark.

Rip, Ruby, Grant, George, and Jennifer filed in and sat down. Exhausted, Jennifer stared at the cold fireplace and let her eyes lose focus as the others chatted. She could still smell smoke in the air.

George, ever the mediator, sought calm. "So, Rip, how was the haying this year?"

Jennifer's father gave him the short answer: "Not bad."

George tried again. "I hear you have a harness horse in training, Grant. Do you have a buyer?"

Grant ducked his head. "Yes, sir."

George paused. "That's wonderful."

At least he'd got a response. It had taken years for Jennifer's brother to warm up to her husband, at least thus far. They'd know Grant was really cozying up to George when he dropped the polite speech. But no one pressured him any more.

Rip filled the gap. "Blevins had to sell off most of his land to the gov'ment. The leftover acres're few enough—what with the cost of running a combine so high these days—that a team or two of Canadians can do the job just fine."

He meant Canadian horses, the tough breed that kept easier than the big drafts and worked just as hard. The market for them was strong. With his son's help, Rip Peterson's second career was proving to be more lucrative than the first. When the local economy shifted with the Grubb years, wheat farmers had been hit hard. The Petersons, too, had been forced to sell off acreage, but the remaining parcel of about one hundred and fifty acres was more than adequate for their purposes now. They'd been able to use their small breeding operation to keep their heads above water and trade grain sales for horse sales.

Ruby broke in. "Dear Lord, must we talk horses? This is our first opportunity to hear news from across the divide. Can we leave the horses out of it?" Her tone was tongue in cheek, but Jennifer knew there was some sincerity to it. "Now, George. Tell us how your work is going."

She would ask him first, Jennifer thought, *and probably last too.* Her mother respected George's quasi-military rank and responsibility far more than her daughter's career focus. She saw her aim to bring high technology to the masses as somehow at odds with God's will, although neither George nor Jennifer had revealed their collaboration in this goal. All Ruby and Rip knew was that George held a high commission trained on urban renewal. And as country folk, they were of the mind that if there was anything needed in the gritty big cities, it was renewal. The role of smart technology in that effort—or the rationale that climate change would force more people to rely on it—was not on Mom and Dad's need-to-know list, Jennifer reminded herself.

George gave them the generic version of what he'd been doing, with Jennifer adding a word or two. They then talked about Chris's and Sabrina's goings-on, and, as Jennifer had anticipated, avoided the topic of her lab work. Just as well.

All the while, Grant sat at a small, carved workbench in one corner of the room, sanding a piece of decorative rock that consumed his attention. Jennifer never knew the man to be idle; she rose and went to see what he was polishing.

At her request, he showed her a curved bar of reddish-brown stone that shone just beneath the rubbed surface. Specks of quartz pocked a design of concentric layers—a beautiful interior, Jennifer knew, that was only hinted at by an outer rough, which looked similar to a regular, old river rock. "Iris agate," she said. "Nice. Where'd you get it?"

Grant returned to his sanding. "Outside Sidney, little pocket of the Yellowstone I know, went there a while back and got totally skunked out, except for this. It was a Monday, and I must've turned over fifty, sixty pound of rock before I come across this one. I ate a ham sandwich for lunch, and I scared up a pheasant, and then when I got home I was late to feed and forgot all about this little beauty. Only then, I remembered. Once I took my hammer to it, there wasn't no doubt."

"It's a keeper," she agreed. "Say. Why don't we go rocking? The kids would probably love to go." She turned to her father. "What do you say, Dad? Can you spare Grant tomorrow or the next day?"

It was rare for Rip—or Grant, or Ruby, for that matter—to take time away from the farm. But Rip had already been considering it.

"I'll spare him tomorrow if he'll fill in for me on Wednesday. Me and George, here, are thinking of playing hooky down at Fort Peck Lake."

"I brought my rod," George put in.

Ruby cleared her throat. "Sheila wants to take the youngsters to the pool down in Miles City one day or the other. But, you men, go ahead and go fishing. And don't let us spoil your plans, Jennifer. You and your brother go off and have a good time."

Jennifer felt some of the tension in her shoulders ease. A day or two free from watching the children would be welcome. She didn't want to leave anyone out, though. "George? Honey? D'you want to bring the kids and come with us?"

He shook his head. "Your mom's right. You and Grant should have some time together. I'll hang out with the rug rats. Besides, if you'll recall the last time you tried to take the kids looking for agates, Sabrina threw a holy fit."

Now Jennifer did remember that day. Her daughter had insisted on taking her shoes off and had cut her foot, ever so slightly, on a rock. She then had to hobble the three-quarters of a mile back to the car, complaining vociferously all the way.

Jennifer cut Grant a look. "Okay. Let's go. First thing tomorrow."

"Okay, Jens. We'll do it." He met her eyes, adding their pet phrase. "Rock and roll."

>>> <<<

Mik was going to have a hell of a shiner where the bumper had hit his calf, but the burns were what really hurt. Again, small price to pay. Nothing like provoking a little sympathy. By dinnertime, his cousins were already speaking to him again.

"Can I see?" Chris moved closer to Mik for a look at his burnt forehead after dessert.

The boy obliged, peeling back a corner of gauze at his temple. Gaps in a welter of puffy blisters showed raw, red skin just inches from Mik's right eye, all of it smeared with a clear ointment.

"Gross. Cool!" Chris said, his earlier cynicism gone.

Sabrina's opinion of her cousin had diminished. "My dad says that something like that won't even leave a scar."

"I've already got scars," Chris bragged, twisting sideways and pulling up the T-shirt he'd put on. Healing-over stripes suggested an attack by a cougar.

Sabrina, sensing he was trying to get a rise out of them, raised her eyebrows and blinked several times. "So?"

Chris's eyes went wide. "How'd you do that?"

"Stepdad," Mik replied, straightening back up.

Sabrina may have felt sorry for him. Still, she couldn't say the right thing. "Maybe you deserved it."

Mik glowered at her, then said acidly, "Maybe I did."

Chris changed the subject. "Your mom lets you start fires?"

Mik threw his head back. "Oh, yeah. Her and Grandpa. Just call me the trash master."

"You burn your—garbage?" Sabrina couldn't quite fathom this. Their household waste went into a chute and, she knew, was automatically separated for usable resources, which went back into the city's maintenance.

"It's legal," Mik said defensively. "Except for a few months in winter."

"Mom said a can exploded in your face," Chris said in awe.

Mik gingerly touched the burnt area. "Yeah, well. Those aren't supposed to go in the pile, but I put 'em there anyway. You rolls the dice, you takes your chances," he added nonchalantly, hoping they wouldn't remember his girly-voice cries.

"Only thing I'm pissed about," Mik went on, "is I can't go to the pool with you guys. The chlorine'd kill me."

Now Sabrina did feel for him. "Miss swimming! I wouldn't wish that on anybody. Even you," she added.

"We swim whenever we want," Chris told his cousin. "There's a Treasure Island pool complex in our pod. It's got a life-sized pirate ship in the middle of it, and a waterfall chute. It's totally noble."

Mik scoffed, "That sounds like its for toddlers."

Sabrina stuck her lip out. "There's also a scuba-diving pool and a shark cage."

That was fuckin' noble.

"Big deal."

Chris didn't notice the sparring that was going on between his cousin and sister. "Yeah, you've got to go down in the shark cage sometime!"

"Are they real sharks?"

"Well, real-ish. They're holograms, but you'd swear they were real," Chris insisted. "You should come visit. Check it out."

Mik thought this over. "Maybe I will," he said. "Maybe I will."

>>> <<<

When Jennifer got up the next morning and went into the kitchen, with Maxi trailing after her, Grant was already making sandwiches. Focused on the task, he wasn't in a talkative mood. She helped load his truck with the food and water, tote bags, and his favorite digging sticks. Then they set off for the short drive to Sidney.

The old Ford left a trail of white smoke, Jennifer saw from the cracked sideview mirror. President Grubb had ripped up the clean-air auto regulations that used to send Grant's truck through periodic emissions tests. Now ensconced in his private, domed island on the country's East Coast, Grubb reaped the windfall from the regulatory tradeoff. The protests over this had died down. Folks in depressed rural areas, like Harmony, were more intent on keeping precious gas in their tanks than worrying about environmental quality—a reality that worked to the administration's advantage.

Jennifer let Maxi perch on her lap, paws on the open window, ears ruffled by the breeze. The smell of moist air sifted in. Grant turned the sputtering truck off the main highway and onto an access road that ran south, to the river.

Jennifer broke the silence. "Don't you want to blindfold me, bro?" The joke was based in truth—local rock hounds could be fierce about protecting their territory.

Grant's lips went slack in his version of a smile. "Just don't tell," he said.

They bumped along until he found what he was looking for, a wide spot in the road shaded by some low-hanging willow trees. He edged the truck as far beneath them as he could. Jennifer wouldn't be surprised if he'd brought a camouflage tarp for further disguise.

Again, comfortable silence settled over them as they geared up and left the parking spot to tramp along the riverbank. Maxi trotted along, nose low to the ground. The cold rush of the watershed and their muted footfalls provided the only sounds. Above the willow and cottonwood on the valley floor rose the distant Rocky range peaks, showing snow at their upper elevations. Beside them, the water in this narrow stretch of the river was low, exposing the alluvial deposits where they would do their hunting. Grant pointed out a blue heron patiently fishing midstream as they passed by.

The further downriver they got, the more like the old days it all seemed. Jennifer felt the stress of her travels rise, hover, and fly off. If only she could capture this moment and place in time, removed as it was from outside influences.

Again Grant motioned as they passed a clump of shrubs, from which a dull cast of aluminum flashed. "My boat," he said of the craft he used for fording the stream when the water was up. Then he stopped short, dropped the lunch pack, and approached the water's edge. Jennifer watched him start poking at the gravel in the dry bar, eyes aimed at the ground.

Practiced at identifying which dull stones might house bright agates, Grant worked swiftly and without distraction, loosening and overturning likely candidates. He discarded most and slipped into his shoulder bag the keepers. These, he would fashion into jewelry or baubles to give away or fill any vacant space in his trailer. In his mud-stained jeans and a gray T-shirt, he blended in, at home among the heron and river rock as Jennifer had once been.

How was it that she'd left this treasure trove for a life that seemed worlds away?

Jennifer began working the gravel bar, recalling that life-changing series of choices. It had all started with the worst fight she'd ever had with her parents, over a college search that, to her, should've ended in a slam-dunk.

Apart from one of her mother's sisters, Delora Lind, Jennifer would be the only other Lind or Peterson, in the U.S., at least, to have pursued higher education. Delora, now long-dead from a traffic crash, had moved to Billings and studied accounting at night while keeping a full-time secretarial job during the day. Her niece had preserved her legacy; Jennifer's grades and ambition in high school earned her near-certain acceptance at many universities.

Her fuzzy goal as a young adult was to study eco-systems, which she'd thought to apply to some sort of

Forest Service or Parks career. A counselor insisted that she try for scholarships at major institutions besides the state U. These efforts all paid off and gave Jennifer the luxury of choice.

She had never shied away from the idea of leaving home, and once faced with undergrad offers from across the country, her ambitions had exploded in scope. She would not even miss her few fellow classmates who were bound for Billings or Missoula. So, one night, she'd informed Rip and Ruby of her decision to accept the MIT full ride and attend college in Massachusetts. A casual observer would have thought she'd been caught digging her parents' graves.

Ruby burst into angry tears and confronted her daughter. "This is the thanks we get?"

Rip played the authoritarian. "Out of state? Out of the question, young lady. You won't get a dime from me to traipse off to that hell hole," meaning, not Cambridge, but Boston—a city he'd never set foot in but one linked with revolution in his mind.

"I won't need your dimes!" Jennifer had retorted. "It's called a scholarship, Dad." She said, condescendingly, "That means they pay for tuition."

This enraged Ruby. "So, now your father's hard-earned money isn't good enough for you?"

If she went to MIT, they predicted, she'd wind up penniless when her money ran out and jailed as a communist dissident.

Their logic escaped Jennifer. "That's what full ride *means:* full room and board, even a stipend for books and things. And, yes, Boston was the seat of revolution—the *American* Revolution, not Russian."

Jennifer couldn't believe her argument for college choice came down to a debate over the Tea Party. "I thought you were for that stuff, not against it," she griped, meaning the far-right, Republican, twenty-first-century version, not the colonial protest.

Her parents had held their ground, until Jennifer headed East in the fall of 2012 and the reality of losing their only daughter to the wider world outside Harmony cracked their resolve. Little by little, they had softened, with Jennifer phoning them again on weekends and Rip sticking a check in the mail now and then.

Originally planning to do field work, Jennifer found that the laboratory atmosphere suited her. Discoveries made by microscope or statistical evaluation became as electrifying to her as finding a rare moss agate. But the real light bulb had switched on when she'd attended a lecture on the burgeoning field of bioengineering.

That this type of research into the human body could actually improve and extend the life of the body tugged at her imagination. It brought back the conversations she'd had with her brother as teenagers, when they'd contemplated the ancient people who had decorated the rock formations in Lakota and Crow country. What if those people could be resurrected—or today's people pre-served—through her work?

To this day, the idea had never left her.

She raised her eyes from the cluster of unremarkable stones at her feet just in time to see Grant thrust his fist in the air and exclaim, "Yes!" He eagerly showed her his find, a dendritic agate that, along with the others, had been formed by volcanic eruption 50 million years in the past.

A sense of connectedness flooded through Jennifer like warm honey, and spread outward to include Grant, the river, a blue-green kingfisher that knifed by. She smiled. It was what persisted that gave life meaning. Her brother knew the value of such things.

CHAPTER 6

Maxi's canine program included a realistic response to the stimuli of new environments, particularly the olfactory ones. She skittered around, sniffing at rotting leaves and other detritus, as far as her virtual leash would let her go. Jennifer and Grant ate their lunch seated on a sandy patch next to the river, leaning against a rock in a comfortable wallow. They had each bagged several pounds of roughs that looked promising. After a lively soliloquy about the specimens he'd looked at and the process involved in deciding whether to keep or discard them, Grant finally turned to his sandwich.

Jennifer had nearly finished hers, plus a bag of chips, an apple, and a part of a bottle of water they were sharing. "I can't tell you how great it is to be on vacation," she said, idly thinking that her brother might not grasp the concept. "I spend my days in a computer lab, not out in the weather with the horses, like you. To make myself feel better, I've got virtual wallpaper in there that I made from a picture you took at Glacier one year. Remember that one with a meadow full of flowering fireweed?"

"July third, 2007," he recited.

"That's the one." *Christ, he's smarter than me*, she marveled.

"Can you make me a virtual wallpaper?"

Jennifer felt like she'd been socked in the gut. "Nooo," she answered slowly. "Your living room would need a serious upgrade." She punched him lightly on the arm. "But you can come see mine. Out West, we've got technology you haven't dreamed of yet."

He swallowed a bite of ham and bread. "Like what?"

Like what. Where to begin?

Her eyes fell on her pet, who had tired of scent hunting and lay down nearby. "Well, take Maxi. You know she's not a real dog; she's a robot."

"I know that."

"Most people in smartcities these days have robotic pets, for better air quality indoors. They're hypoallergenic, and less hassle. You never have to feed 'em, or brush 'em, or take them to the vet. You can use them as trash compactors or program in tricks."

"Banjo can't do any of that. Do they fart?" Grant asked seriously.

"There's an app for that," she said lightly. "No joke. You can enable simulated bodily functions, if you're into that kind of thing."

Then she described the augmented reality displays that she and George and the kids relied on for everything from research to homework and entertainment. She told him about how robotics and 3-D printing had made crafting and building things quicker and cheaper. "Some of this stuff is in the works, but a lot of it is out in the world already."

"Not my world," he said ruefully.

"That's the thing, Grant. It's not just your world. Or President Grubb's world, or the Western Land Core's world. It's our world."

This statement of inclusion seemed to bring him great pleasure. "*Our* world," he repeated grandly. Then he scowled and said darkly, "The government is rot."

"This… *gift*… shouldn't belong to the government," Jennifer agreed. "That's what George and I are working on: bringing the gift of science to all the people. If one can't have it, nobody should."

She went on to tell him how she expected artificial intelligence to advance other forms of technology, such as bioengineering, to make sick people well, and to help them live longer by replacing worn-out body parts. "You know, like how pacemakers keep hearts pumping, or plastic joints can replace bad knees."

"Could they even make new brains?"

Jennifer wondered how candid she should be. "In a way," she answered. "They'll give us new ways to share information. Someday, we'll succeed in making machines that are smarter than us." *Like, next week, hopefully,* she added, to herself.

He pondered this. "If they're smarter than us, will they be nicer than us?"

A thrill shot through Jennifer. She glanced at her brother, impressed again by his ability to run down a topic to its very core. He got it. For a guy who'd been teased and downright abused mercilessly as a kid, humane treatment was a priority. The choice to embrace it *was* what made us human. And the backlash in the past dozen years had been based on fears that independent thinking machines would lack such restraint, and seek to obliterate their creators.

"They will be nicer," she promised, "because they'll be more perfect." She paused. "Think about it, Grant. These devices will have all the information on Earth. We'll be the ones to give it to them. Would this make them want to harm us? No. They would be profoundly grateful."

"They'd say thanks," he translated.

"Not just that. If they have everything they need to know, and a high regard for their 'architects,' they'll have a special kind of... love, I'd call it. Like, the kind that stops wars. The kind that can bring us together."

"So you could come back home."

This touched her.

"So we'd all *be* home. All the time."

Another kingfisher flew by, headed upstream, its staccato cries breaking the mood. Maxi jumped to her feet, barking.

Jennifer slapped Grant's thigh and began gathering up the food wrappers. "I'm getting stiff. Let's get back to work."

>>> <<<

The hours out in the sun wore out the threesome, in a good way. Jennifer hadn't felt so happily tired in a long time. *I need to get more exercise,* she thought. *And more sun. And more... "me" time.* Grant, who was used to long days, found conversation, even with his sister, draining. And Maxi had managed to tucker herself out—no mean feat for a robotic dog—and was nearly sapped of energy by late afternoon, when they returned to the truck. Jennifer made a note to recharge her when they got back to the farm.

This she did, propping her pet up on the dashboard pad that wirelessly replenished all of the family's phones and devices. She also fulfilled her own request for exercise and time alone the next day, while her mother and sister took the kids swimming and her father and husband spent the day fishing. Watching Grant patiently put one of his fillies through early harness training in one of the flat paddocks, she got the urge to ride out on the property on horseback.

The family always kept a saddle horse or two for riding fences, or these days, for the odd trip to town, to save on gas. Jennifer asked Grant which mount would be best for her.

"Take old Madeline," he said, waving to one of the pastures.

She left her brother striding behind the young mare in harness. He guided the horse with two long reins as she dragged a short length of log from the singletree, to get her used to pulling and being followed. Grant had obviously earned her trust.

Madeline, a black horse whose summer coat had faded to brown, proved difficult to catch at first. But when Jennifer didn't let up with her dogged foot chase, the twenty-something mare at last turned and faced her, resigned.

Jennifer slipped a halter over her nose and led her out of the mares' pasture and into the stable for saddling.

Time frayed at its edges as the horse and rider moved out over the farm's open land, across the flat area nearest the stable yard that was used for driving and into the gentle hills that ran toward the edge of the property. Jennifer swiftly lost the internal dialogue that narrated each day, the minutiae of things to do and worry about that normally kept up a dull chatter in her head. Like glassblowing, riding took her out of herself, exposed her roots, the way George's sitting meditation or Grant's rock polishing did for them.

As the noonday sun warmed her skin, Jennifer listened to Madeline's faint blowing, watched her shoulder muscles pump and sway, felt her own seat bones rise and fall in the saddle. A shadow crossed over them, and Jennifer raised her eyes to spy the silhouette of red-tailed hawk, silently circling upward. She would have meandered along indefinitely had she and her horse not reached the fence boundary, an unfamiliar post-and-wire barrier that marked the farm's newly abbreviated property line.

Madeline obliged the squeeze of her rider's knees against the saddle and palms against the reins, and stopped. A brief wave of sadness hit Jennifer in the chest. She tried to slough it off. *Nothing lasts forever,* she chided herself. At least the family farm was still somewhat intact, and her father and brother were making a decent living from it.

But the shrinking of what had once seemed limitless affected her now, a sense of frustration and loss she hadn't felt this deeply since that day she'd run from the funding meeting, thinking her research dead in the water.

"Yeah, and you were wrong," she nagged herself aloud. "Look how that turned out." She might not have reached her goal, but it was still alive, and she'd made progress. A small smile lifted her lips as she recalled the way she'd described the episode to her lab computer, Jack16. Failure didn't erase a problem; it preserved it. It was still there for the solving. *All I have to do now is find a new angle.*

She chirruped to Madeline and reined her back toward the barn.

>>> <<<

George surprised himself with his reluctance to leave Harmony as the visit came to a close. Five days of togetherness with his wife's family was usually plenty for him. They made an effort to include him, but his heritage kept him ever the outsider. It went beyond skin tone— for Jennifer's brother and father, whose days in the sun and wind altered their light, Scandinavian coloring, were nearly as dark as he was. And it went beyond his birthplace of Monterey—for although the elder Petersons considered California "out there," they considered Mexico, the land of his forebears, beyond the bounds of civilization.

Much of this prejudice could be attributed to Grubbist rhetoric, of which they'd partaken a steady diet since the first set of isolationist presidential campaigns. Back then, George had laughed off the pledge to wall off the United States from its south-of-the-border neighbor. "We'll just sail around it," he'd joked to his brother Gilberto. Before emigrating north, their ancestors had run a shipping enterprise between La Paz and Monterey, back when Baja and Alta California had traded ownership between the Spanish and Mexican governments.

Xical family members also joked about their blended history, as theories and tall tales abounded as to how their Aztec and Spanish relations had first allied in marriage. Many of these accounts conflicted, and none had ever been proven. And now, they likely never would be. George and Gilberto had lost both parents, their remaining *abuela*, and two brothers in Grubb's short-lived southern war, in 2020. It had been this epic failure that had prompted modern-day California—its citizens already dismayed by Grubb's election to the presidency—to secede from the United States. Having backed Mexico, not the U.S., in the conflict, the state would likely have been the target of civil war next, had not more pressing global matters consumed the Grubb administration's resources and focus. When Oregon and Washington separated as well, followed by Nevada and Arizona, the Western Land Core had been born.

In the eight years since, profound pain and healing had mingled. Former Americans in the West had to contend with family living east of the divide—the national border now being defined by the states' previous eastern boundaries. Tensions had not yet fully eased, and in some cases, never would. Westerners who had sided with Mexico in the trade-driven war were seen as traitors to America, even though they had been loyal to American ideals of free enterprise and diplomacy. Those who remained in what would later become the Ameristates were viewed as misguided as best, and backward and cowardly at worst. The division took its toll, causing even George and his brother, Gilberto, to drift apart.

Having sustained so much familial loss of life himself, George had, after a time, swapped laying blame for building a new homeland. He and Gilberto had survived, after all, by lending their skills to defense of their native country. The California guard had benefited from their deft ability to move people and supplies where they were needed. They were duly rewarded with WLC posts. It was in this capacity that George had found common cause with his wife's altruistic goals. So, in a way, the Second Mexican War had, despite George's personal losses, brought him and Jennifer closer together.

This might have been the biggest sticking point with Rip and Ruby, he suspected. All during Jennifer's scholarly years—as she matriculated her way from MIT to University of Chicago to Stanford—they'd cultivated the hope of her eventual return. Even when she married George, became pregnant with Chris, and then Sabrina, they'd somehow imagined that she would see the light, leave the godforsaken West, and move back to Harmony, Montana. It may have been, to their minds, George's fault that she did not.

So it was, generally, with some relief that George's annual visit to Jennifer's clan ended and he went back to the Olympic Cities, where they had both been transferred a few years after the war. But today, George felt unusually content here, and loath to get back in the car tomorrow and say good-bye. Perhaps it was just the long drive ahead, or the rapport he'd enjoyed with Rip while fishing the other day. Or maybe it was hanging out in the cozy, old stable now as a late-summer thunderstorm pelted outside. Whatever the reason, he was enjoying an easiness with Jennifer's relatives that he often feigned, but that rarely actually surfaced.

George, Chris, and Sheila's boy, Mik, lounged lazily in the main barn, killing time, while Rip and Grant shod their stallion, a stocky little bay horse with two white socks. The barn door stood open, and Rip bent over the hoof stand while Grant held the horse steady beneath the overhang. A compact gas forge nearby put out enough heat to be welcome and enough noise to limit conversation. As Rip used tongs to align a hot steel shoe with the stallion's hoof wall, the smell of scorched keratin permeated the wet air. Satisfied with the shape, he cooled the shoe in a water bucket and proceeded to nail it on. The final peg slipped from his fingers.

"Damn. Hand me that nail, would you?" Rip called to George, without taking his eyes off of the hoof he was tending. The dull roar of the forge and the steady gush of rain overrode any sound that might have come from a steel nail hitting the dirt floor of the barn. George bent and retrieved the nail for Rip, who grunted under the strain of his work.

Chris and Mik hung back from the drafty doorway. George watched them begin a casual target practice, attempting to knock over a row of bottles with whatever projectiles they could find on the barn floor. Rip finished with the stallion, brushing his hands on his leather apron. George watched Grant lead the animal away to his stall and return to sweep up.

Rip switched off the forge. Outside, the cloudburst had dwindled to a swift drizzle. Suddenly, George could hear himself think again.

"Nice work," he complimented his father-in-law.

Rip was too modest or inured to the task to acknowledge this. He bent and moved the hoof stand to a corner. Again he groaned, and put a hand to his back as he straightened up. "I'm gettin' too old for this," he lamented. "Wish there was an easier way."

"Told you I'd do it," Grant said, then he had an idea. "Hey, maybe that God machine Jens is working on'll be able to shoe horses."

Plink! Mik knocked a bottle over with a rusty lug nut and glanced their way. "A what machine?"

Grant continued sweeping up hoof trimmings. "It's this computer/robot thing that's supposed to be a trillion times smarter than any human. It'll be able to stop wars and make people live forever, and it'll be super nice too. So maybe it'll be able to do horseshoeing, and prob'ly even the haying, and anything else you and me don't want to do, Pop," he said, ignoring Mik. "The more it knows, the more perfect it'll be. And maybe it'll get so perfect, it'll take the place of God one day."

He seemed to be babbling, but he'd snagged Rip's attention. "Do what now? Stoppin' wars and baling hay and what-all?" To himself, he said, "Never know what that gal'll get up to." He thought a moment, then said to Grant, "Good Lord, son. Do not mention none of this to your mother."

Or to anyone else, George thought, uneasily. He saw that the topic had attracted Mik's interest as well. The teenager had left Chris taking potshots at bottles and come over to help Grant search the floor for errant nails.

"You get ahold of a farrier robot and we could make a million dollars," he said.

"Pshaw," countered his grandfather. "Work's work. Always will be. That's where dollars come from. As my mother used to say, a pie on the table is worth ten in the sky. Am I right?" He grinned at George, whom he considered a stabilizing influence on his imaginative daughter.

George nodded.

>>> <<<

Jennifer, too, was having separation pangs when it came time to leave on Saturday morning, at sunrise. She felt her old routine loom as she exhorted Chris and Sabrina to double-check their guestroom for belongings. Ruby brought forth a sack of snacks she'd put together. Rip and Grant had put off the feeding chores long enough to see them off, and hovered in the front yard.

Mik appeared somewhat aggrieved at having been pulled out of bed and marched into line with his mother and little sister to say good-bye to his cousins and the adults. Jennifer gave him credit, though. As Chris continually reminded her, growing boys loved their sleep.

She gathered up an armload of bags and offered to bring the car around. Just then, she stopped short. "Oh, shit!" Nobody noticed as she hustled to the carport, anxiety rising.

The sedan hadn't been used since its unscheduled trip, and Jennifer had left Maxi charging in it after their day on the river. Maybe she'd relaxed *too* much.

She set down her cargo, relieved to find Maxi still lying peacefully on the dashboard, feeding from the energy pad. "Hey, girl," she said fondly, syncing the dog's collar to her bracelet and releasing her pet. Maxi sniffed the air, catching a scent, and trotted away.

Jennifer put her stuff in the trunk and shut it, then got in the driver's seat and backed the car out and into the yard. Slight chaos ensued as George tried to store everything amid the well wishes and warnings from Ruby, Rip, and Sheila. Mik and Lizzie had gone back to bed.

At last, Chris and Sabrina climbed back into the backseat, and Jennifer accepted one more bear-crushing hug from Grant before taking the wheel. George slipped into the passenger seat beside her. She checked over her shoulder to see that the kids weren't fighting yet… and noticed that Maxi was not in back with them.

She threw a lightning glance at George, and then wrenched the door open and stumbled out. "Maxi!" she yelled at the top of her voice. "Maxi, come!"

Jennifer looked wildly around the front yard, patting her bracelet. She could've sworn she'd synced up with her pet. *Must be something wrong with the leash function.* "Has anybody seen Maxi?"

The frantic note in her voice brought reassurance from Ruby. "Let's have a look, dear. We'll find her."

Rip chimed in, "We won't let you go home without her."

Jennifer gritted her teeth, thinking, *You're goddamned right you won't.*

CHAPTER 7

The delay of twenty hours on the road plus a motel layover was almost more than Jennifer could stand. Yes, they'd found Maxi sniffing about the manure spreader, cleaned her up, and begun their trip home. But what had allowed the robotic pet to take off with the precious data files? Had it been a functional glitch? Or something more? This was no time for conjecture. Jennifer needed answers now.

She left her tired family to unpack and unwind after arriving at the home pod in midafternoon, and took the pedway to her laboratory in the adjoining OC-4 complex. A physical retractable leash tethered her to the renegade dog. As Maxi strained at the lead, a passerby joked, "Are you walking that dog, or is it walking you?" Jennifer grinned feebly. The cliché question, in this instance, was a valid one.

She couldn't shrug off the sensation that something—or someone—was behind the near-disastrous glitch. If she'd lost those files… It wasn't just her body of research that was at risk. The outcome she sought—a human-level thinking apparatus tempered by a sense of justice and compassion—could positively affect the entire world population. Not just today's people, but all of their descendants. *No pressure,* she thought wryly, shaking her head.

The pair made their way past the robotic guard and through the maze of secured doors to Jennifer's lab. Her furtive glances over her shoulder were hardly necessary. Time off was strictly encouraged, and this being Sunday and the end of the holiday week, only a few die-hards haunted the building. Besides, the identity scanner allowed just two people to enter the computer bank— Jennifer and her boss, James Ting. Limited access was meant to safeguard both the data and the hardware. At this point, though, Jennifer wasn't sure stringent clearance would be enough.

At least it offered privacy. She switched off Maxi's main program and began a thorough diagnostic scan. Then she sat back to let the program run through several hundred million lines of self-generated code. This gave her more than enough time to think. Jennifer's eyes fixed on the red and blue flashing lights on the dog's collar. Her peripheral vision faded as her worries floated to the surface.

What next? She'd returned to the lab fully intending to restore Val2001's hard-drive content before Ting or anyone else found out that she'd nicked it. But wouldn't the material be safer under her own protection?…considering it represented the aggregate of her dozen years of hard work. And considering she'd be a hell of a lot more careful from now on. This rationale lacked strict adherence to department codes, she knew.

Jennifer glanced over at her assistant, the small pebble that housed Jack16. "Maybe I should let you run it through Ethics," she joshed the dormant machine.

The tests took forever, but Jennifer stayed. Despite the iris scanner and two-step locking procedure, she wasn't convinced that Maxi would be safe overnight in the unmanned lab. At last, the lights on the dog's collar stopped flickering, and she could bring up the results on her desk interface.

The analysis showed a file corruption in Maxi's leash function, but whether it was due to a registry error or a coding glitch was unclear. Of greater interest was the readout of Maxi's hard drive, which she'd transferred in full from Val's unit. Jennifer's mouth dropped open. The dog's memory was nearly full.

The most recent scan had shown Val's remaining capacity at 35 percent. Given the projected volume and pace of work, it should have taken another six months to exhaust that. Where had more raw data come from?

Jennifer wracked her brain, trying to remember whether she'd performed any quantitative uploads off-grid. She couldn't think of any. And since she'd swiped the files before vacation, she couldn't blame Ting.

Holy shit!

The car.

Maxi was connected to the automobile's computer while on the charging pad. But the exchange had only been meant to boost her energy cells—not to transmit anything other than the charging data, so as not to drain the car's battery completely. Was it possible for the robot to *request* information?

A shiver went down Jennifer's spine, and she staggered to her feet. Still short on answers, she needed to buy some time. And she couldn't risk the dog running off again. She rummaged through the supply cupboard until she found what she was looking for, a security implant used for the building's robotic guard force, much like the ones that would prevent child kidnapping or intelligence harvesting. Even if someone found the drive, they'd be unable to access it without the two-factor biometric password she would configure. Of course, if her boss learned of the ploy, she'd have a lot of explaining to do… and excuses probably wouldn't do her much good. Theoretically, at least, the government lab did own the information.

Jennifer hesitated, but only for a moment.

The hell with it, she decided. She'd bring the dog—and the data—home. And everywhere else she had to go. In other words, she chose to violate protocol, her engineer's oath of compliance, and national law, in order to keep the files under her own protection.

Jennifer checked the time. It was late—past dinnertime. But George would understand. She removed Maxi's face plate and went to work. She wasn't taking any more chances.

>>> <<<

"Did you read this, Jenny? Hawaii has formally cut ties with Ameristates." George sat at the glass breakfast table that hung from the ceiling, scanning the news on his glistening electronic paper. After the vacation, the family had fallen back into their routine. Now, some three weeks later, the holiday break seemed distant and their daily schedules once again encompassed them.

Jennifer dabbed some more jam on her breakfast pizza. "Way to go, Hawaii! About time," she said. "Is there a chance of folding them into the WLC?" The archipelago's strategic location had long been jealously guarded by the old U.S. republic. Then, military-industrial interests had sought to privatize the state and profit from its naval bases. But Hawaiian leaders had resisted.

"There's no doubt it would bolster our physical presence globally," George reasoned. "But that's not absolutely necessary. A strong alliance might do us just as much good. We don't need Honolulu as missile base. Our long-range drones are plenty effective." He sipped from a green drink and swallowed. "Anyway, it says here that independence is the present goal. How exciting is that for what's left of the native population?"

Jennifer nodded, wondering idly what it would be like for Montanans to rule themselves. News of a new island nation begged the question of whether more of Grubb's "corporate states" would opt out after the bogus vote that gave the Ameristates leader an unprecedented third term—or whether outright civil war would have to happen first. The contiguous states were in no hurry to repeat the conflict that had come about after the Mexican trade war escalated into combat, followed by the California uprising. They would carefully weigh the cons of war against the pros of sovereignty—and current widespread economic depression raised the stakes in gambling with both durable and human resources.

George read aloud, "'Hawaii's possession of a sizable Ameristates' arsenal is expected to render the split conclusive, without any opposition by the Grubb administration.' Wow."

"If only we had been so lucky." Jennifer noted that the islands' remote position in the Pacific Ocean contributed to the possibility of a bloodless secession. "If Cali hadn't been forced to take sides sooner than later, we might've been able to negotiate the same sort of split, with no harm done. If only we'd been so lucky," she repeated.

"Second that," George said soberly, glancing at his son and daughter across the table. George believed in choosing positives over negatives. When faced with reminders of his Mexican and Californian relations who'd sacrificed their lives in the war, he forced himself to think of the future. "Chris, *¿qué vas a hacer hoy?* Can we fit in a jam session this afternoon?"

Chris paused the action/adventure he was experiencing and raised his smartglasses. "Maybe tonight, Dad."

"Brin? How about you?"

Sabrina, somewhere deep in solving a math problem, either didn't hear him or purposely ignored him. She stared off into space through her glasses.

"We've got a date at Mena's after school today," Jennifer explained. She often visited friends or took the kids and Maxi out on Tuesdays. Today she'd combine those activities, meeting Philomena for coffee while Chris and Sabrina sailed around OC-5, the canal city.

George acknowledged this plan and set down his empty drink cup. Jennifer and Chris pushed back their plates. Sabrina's lack of interest indicated that she'd finished her breakfast as well.

Oooh-ooo, oooh-ooo! whined Maxi from beneath the table.

Through the glass, Jennifer met her gray eyes, the products of her security implant. She'd programmed the dog to beg when everyone was done eating.

Maxi twirled on her hind legs and sat back down, looking expectant.

"Good girl. Recycle mode." Jennifer scraped the plates and emptied the scraps into the dog's mouth.

"Should I take her out before school?" Chris asked. He had his mother's efficiency gene and tended to do his chores early, so he could relax later.

"No—negative. I'll take care of it," Jennifer said, trying to think of a reason to keep the dog close. "No more trash duty until further notice. I'm… monitoring Maxi for worms." Pets were often the targets of malicious computer viruses.

"Alright!" Chris jumped up and sank an imaginary basket.

Sabrina lifted her glasses. "Any chores you don't want me to do, Mom?"

She had been listening. Jennifer just frowned.

George lingered at the table. "I'm not looking forward to plugging in today. We're getting some blowback on City Access from that Jesus group."

"Funny how what's sacred suddenly becomes a matter of money when you call people on it," Jennifer said with bare sarcasm.

"I know. First it's their religious rights, then it's their profits. Even though there's no wiggle room legally, they'll take the opportunity to sound off. Come to think of it, I might not be done until dinner anyway." Tuesdays were George's meeting days. He kissed his wife and left for the early shift in his office down the hall.

>>> <<<

Several hours later, Jennifer and Philomena sat chatting on the verandah of an open-air café, with their dogs seated at their feet. Philomena's robotic pet was a black-and-white border collie with dark speckles on its paws, slightly taller and thinner than Maxi. The café balcony overlooked an active, yet tranquil, canal thoroughfare. Self-guided gondolas cruised past below, ferrying passengers and freight in two directions. A funky, flat odor rose from discreetly placed vents, piped in to add ambience to the manufactured waterway. It had the feel and grandeur of Old Venice, and would have to do as a substitute, since the Italian city had at last succumbed to rising sea levels.

Chris and Sabrina couldn't get enough of the unlimited ride time, and they'd gone off exploring, safe enough in the fully enclosed city. State-of-the-art OC-5 was a prototype for environmental engineering, with a virtual, smart nanomaterial containing its atmosphere and regulating its weather programming. Jennifer sat back, relishing the time to relax with her friend and talk over important issues.

Philomena Fine employed a healthy skepticism, no matter what the topic—a trait that served her well as a jurist. "Get the fuck out!" she exclaimed now, spraying pastry crumbs over the table and her purple dress suit. She choked a bit and washed down the unswallowed portion with a carbonated espresso drink.

"I shit you not, Mena," Jennifer assured her, flicking a few crumbs from the sleeve of her fleece sweater. "Protest rallies and everything."

Philomena had asked how George's grand openings were going at the public housing. Most of the new buildings had been lauded by the press and public-welfare groups. But a few, in the more conservative WLC territories, had become the subjects of political argument.

"I hate to say this,"—Philomena's tone of voice showed that it didn't really bother her to say it—"but there's the door." She upended her drink and burped, then patted her chest. "First rule? Abide by the majority. You don't like that rule, tough titties. There's really not much more to debate. They're certainly free to leave."

Jennifer raised her eyebrows and nodded tiredly. "You know it, I know it. It's called a social contract." She raised her coffee cup to her lips, but it was empty, and she set it back down. "Sure, people who voted for Grubb were trapped here after the war. They weren't welcome in Grubbland, and they didn't want to become refugees elsewhere. And now they want what they used to have...."

"The right to legislate their beliefs," Mena supplied. "I don't think so. That's what they *thought* was theirs. Not so, even in the old America. They stole that right, or paid off their reps to steal it." She took another bite of pastry and swallowed more carefully this time. "Not what the Founding Fathers had in mind. Ben Franklin himself held that any religion worth its salt would be strong enough to stand on its own. In fact, he said seeking legitimacy from the courts was proof enough of a false doctrine."

Leave it to Philomena to find an example from history to illustrate a point. The woman had spent an entire lifetime studying American history, and was now on her second lifetime—as she referred to the WLC era—intent on applying that wisdom to the new national framework.

Jennifer met her gaze. Mena's clear, brown eyes reflected passion, reason, and a lack of reverence. Even at her most vehement, she gave the impression that all the world was a stage. Yet, she held herself—and others—to high standards when it came to justice and equality. Doubt was simply her tool for extorting proof. Wild around the edges though she was, her judicious nature leaked into her demeanor, perhaps compelling her to style her crinkled, silver-gray hair in a bun and to persist in using old-fashioned reading glasses when everyone else simply had corrective nanosurgery. But the upswept hair tended to escape its bonds throughout the day, and the glasses were often used as a foil for her ability to unequivocally assess a given situation. In heated discourse, if Judge Fine sat forward and perched her glasses on her nose, she was not readying for a second guess; she was about to read someone the riot act.

"So, how's George taking all this?" her friend pressed, meaning the resurgence of church-and-state bickering.

"Better than you are," Jennifer kidded. "Nah, you know he's more... accepting of these things. While still knowing where to draw the line."

"The line is crystal clear! 'Matters of religion shall be wholly separate from matters of state, and, in the event their interests overlap, those of the state shall take priority.'"

Her friend could quote the national charter, that was for sure. And Jennifer loved her for it. It wasn't often that the concerns of science and governance were upheld without prejudice. Philomena Fine embodied the notion.

Jennifer hailed the roving waiterbot and ordered two sweepers—drinks that counteracted the effects of caffeine—so that she and Mena could enjoy as much more coffee as they liked, until Chris and Sabrina came back to meet their curfew. And this conversation deserved the full Fine treatment. Jennifer, too, had been indignant, though not surprised, by the conservative city groups' objections to implementing the public-housing law. The clash had come when religious-themed cities were obliged to accept new inhabitants—residents who were *not* obligated to accept new belief systems. When the cities were still private entities, tenants were within their rights to impose a religious theme. But now that every WLC city was legally bound to include public housing, those themes that violated charter law were no longer sanctioned. The "Jesus group" that George had mentioned was contending a large loss on its theme investment.

"Yes, free-speech protest is protected," Philomena went on. "But state law supersedes religious expression. Case closed."

"It's what's great about the WLC," Jennifer said. "In preserving all spiritual freedoms, no one religion may be favored. I'm perfectly willing to accept that."

Philomena grinned. "You're willing to keep your atheism to yourself in order to protect your right not to believe in that other shit," she summed up.

"And vice versa. I say, go ahead and delude yourself all you want, people. Just don't foist it off on anyone else."

"*That*," Mena pointed out, "is exactly what John Adams would have said, but in more colloquial terms. I would go a step further and contend that belief in hocus pocus actively holds the human race back from reaching its full potential. Think back to when folks believed black cats and broken mirrors and the number thirteen brought bad luck. Superstitious nonsense, which we got over. Rational thought: it's not like it can't be done."

"I'm with you there. I used to wonder why it seemed that evolution had slowed, or plateaued, or stopped altogether. The truth is that it hasn't; it's just that our misperceptions run so deep they make it seem so."

"It's hard to get the big picture when you're standing right in the thick of it," Mena observed.

Jennifer nodded. "I stand as the poster child for objective study. I'm convinced a species break-up is coming. The question is, who'll be on what side?"

"Well, we know which side you'll be on. What about George?"

Jennifer paused. What *about* George?

"We're on the same page," she finally answered. At least, she thought so. Compromise had not been Jennifer's strong suit, at first. It had taken a few years of sporadic negotiation and living through the trials of war together to straighten things out between them. A marriage ran much better on shared priorities, and she had to hand it to George for letting her figure that out on her own.

She remembered his reaction the first time she'd mentioned her spiritual beliefs. His facial expression was firmly etched in her mind: a perfect mosaic of surprise and respect, confusion and understanding. He'd been either so shocked or so intrigued—or both—that he had listened just long enough to work up to a juicy argument.

They'd met at the start of the university term back in 2015, as Jennifer was embarking on her doctoral track and George was immersed in graduate work in economics. He had paused his education after high school to travel, and had spent eight years bouncing between sleepy coastal villages and the family business. He'd work in the office awhile and then hit the road, only to return when his funds ran out. Eventually, he'd awakened to the course of study that seemed right, and was accepted by Stanford University. He and Jennifer had crossed paths in an economics justice class, and they could often be found on campus, discussing their theories late into the night.

One evening, seated on a bench, under a tree outside Landau Hall, Jennifer felt comfortable enough with George to disclose personal ideas that she rarely shared. The question of whether ethics should even be a part of economic theory had come up in class. They'd been ruminating over the topic together.

"What's so wrong about trying to correct the main problem with money?" Jennifer had asked. "Without a moral framework, numbers are harsh and cruel."

George agreed. "One man's largesse is another man's poverty."

"The whole 'economic survival of the fittest' thing comes down to basics," Jennifer said, her passion rising. "Why are we here? Where are we going?"

"And shouldn't we all be going together, as a human race?" George added, expecting her to be onboard with that. "How else will we survive?"

Jennifer drew back slightly and dropped her gaze. "Well, it could be that only the strong among men *will* survive. And by 'strong,' I mean 'smart.' In future terms, strength will correlate to intelligence, and intelligence will outstrip the limits of our puny brains. We're already well down the road of creating bigger problems for our planet than we can solve. I believe we'll need to merge with machines just to move forward, to endure, to evolve."

He gave her a hard look. "A lot of people won't swallow that idea."

"Denying a fact doesn't make it disappear. Reasonable people will accept it." Her confidence was laced with arrogance. "So, maybe a divergence is crucial to a human future."

It was George's turn to recoil. "What're you saying? That we'll have to leave behind our humanity for some Darwinian upgrade?"

Jennifer knit her brow, exasperated. He sounded like the other doubters she knew who'd grappled with this concept. "We'll leave behind our human foibles—not our humanity," she corrected him. "Listen, Xical. What tanks logical thought? Huh? *Irrational* thought. Beliefs based on emotions, misunderstandings, fantasies, and lies. Until we dump that stuff, we'll just be spinning our wheels."

"But we all have our inherent biases. As a scientist, you know that," he scolded her.

"Sure. But deep down, we *know* our prejudices. Even try to overcome them. I'm talking about willful ignorance, or wishful thinking."

"You mean, like politics? Or religion?"

She barked a short laugh. "Both. People buy into them, based on selfish whims. Those two frameworks capitalize on emotions to sway our thinking. And that divides us— far more than church services or campaign rallies bring us together. We say those things do, but they don't." She realized this sounded harsh and asked, more meekly, "*You* don't believe they do; do you?"

"Well, I believe in civic duty, and just laws. But partisanship? What's the point?" George seemed to look inside himself. "And I am not one for organized religion, if that's what you're asking. No."

She heaved an inward sigh of relief.

He tilted his chin. "But billions of people are, Jennifer. And I do believe in a life of the soul. So, which beliefs are we entitled to?"

"The ones based in reality," she replied stubbornly. "Not that things have to be seen to be real—I consider myself spiritual when I connect with nature, with my thoughts and feelings. This is what brings us to a higher consciousness. Not prayers and so-called holy books."

"You're saying that all those people of faith have to sacrifice their worldviews in order to move up the food chain?"

"In a word, yes." She registered his silence as disapproval. "It's inevitable, don't you see? Those who don't make the leap and enhance their capacity with the vast information that computers will be able to access will eventually die out."

"Survival of the fittest," he pronounced sarcastically.

She shrugged. "Hey, it's not my rule. Nature will cull the herd, so to speak. The remaining population will be of a manageable size, with enough resources and regard for each other to unite forever. For the good of the species."

George squirmed. "*Ay, ay, ay,* woman. You're willing to sacrifice a major chunk of humanity so the rest can be… perfect?"

"I'm just saying, people will not give up their Bibles or Qurans, or even blind trust in reincarnation, or the void, or dumb luck. They're too obstinate, or immersed in groupthink. It would be sad for billions of people to be too bull-headed to evolve, but I don't see any way around it."

"So, the majority of people can't change," George interpreted with irony.

"Not can't. Won't."

He had no rejoinder for this.

Jennifer watched something thick and sorrowful flood George's dark eyes. They had broken off their talk, uneasy and unsatisfied, without proposing another date.

They'ad gotten back together and found enough fuel to ignite their passion, soon marrying, and swiftly producing their first child. But the relationship still needed a guiding light—a unifying principle. Had it not been for her father's surprising turnaround not long after Chris was born, Jennifer might never have come around to George's optimistic take on human nature.

"Superstition, rational thought… it all comes down to free will," she told Philomena now. "And open eyes. Take my dad, for instance. Here's a man who never missed a church service—even during haying. When things went wrong, when I was little, he'd say it was God's will. And when they went right, ditto."

"Abrogating his own responsibility," Philomena put in.

"But during the first Grubb campaign, when all that shit was coming out about what an amoral creep he was, *while* he was pandering to the evangelicals, Dad finally wised up. The big guys he idolized kept saying that God was choosing a 'flawed man' as his servant, that no matter how low Grubb was, he was destined to do God's will— "

"Mainly because he promised them the legislation, and the money and power that they wanted," Mena concluded.

"Right," Jennifer said. "But Dad believed in those values—sanctity of marriage, virtuous living, doing unto others. He saw the fundamental disconnect and decided there had to be a better servant than that—one who was married umpteen times, who was lecherous and who would turn his back on the poor."

"Whoa." Philomena was impressed. "What'd he do?"

"He stood up in church and pointed out the hypocrisy. He quit watching the televangelists. He even voted Blue. I'd never been so proud of him in my life."

Mena took this in. "What'd your mother think about that?"

"She about had a cow." They'd ordered another couple of espressos, and Jennifer stopped to sip some more. She set her cup down and twisted it to and fro by the handle. "But here's where Dad practices what he preaches—and why George loves him, I'm sure," she added. "He let Mom have her beliefs. He didn't try to argue her out of them. He gave his reasons for what he was doing—but he didn't try to judge her. Or change her."

"… And, let me guess: she voted for Grubb."

"She did." A dull ache spread inside as she recalled that election. The aftermath had been devastating. "And I couldn't talk to her for a long time. Frankly, Dad was a lot more forgiving than me. Hell, he had to live in the same house with her. Or, he didn't have to—he chose to. It could've ended his marriage." She took another sip of coffee, remembering how that display of personal generosity had struck her and stayed with her. "So, yeah," she continued. "Free will. It might be our saving grace. Rather than being bound by a mutation or some other accident of evolution, we'll be able to choose to embrace our future." She had discussed this with George at the time, and allowed that she'd been short-sighted in giving up on people before they'd had a chance to make their decisions.

She noticed Chris and Sabrina coming up the causeway and gathered her things to go. The dogs took this as a signal to rise and stretch. "So, I learned something, Mena. From the Christians. Put that in your pipe and smoke it."

Philomena pushed her chair back and regarded her friend, bemused. "I'm not sure that's the high I'm looking for."

PART II

WASHINGTON (AP) – PRESIDENT GRUBB SUFFERS HEART ATTACK, THIRD-TERM INAUGURATION POSTPONED

Tuesday President Harold Grubb was rushed to surgery following a life-threatening myocardial infarction. A spokesman said he is stable and in recovery. The inauguration ceremony slated for Sunday has been postponed, with no date set...

WASHINGTON (AP) – GRUBB ON LIFE SUPPORT, PRESIDENCY IN LIMBO

WASHINGTON (AP) – HAROLD GRUBB JR. SWORN IN AS 2ND AMERISTATES PRESIDENT

SEQUOIA (AP) – AMERISTATES BANS ALL TRAVEL NOT RELATED TO TRADE

Washington confirmed an immediate ban on travel to and from Ameristates by foreign nationals and Ameristates citizens for any purpose unrelated to business transactions. The move has drawn widespread condemnation from WLC leaders...

CHAPTER 8

February 12, 2030

"Da-ad," Sabrina wailed. "Do we have to?"

A day at the soup kitchen: oh, boy. Why couldn't Saturdays be more pleasant? A kid buckled down all week and did as the parents commanded… and then along came Saturday. Dad was all, *Community outreach!* And Mom was like, *Think of how much you'll learn.*

Learn?

Saturday was when learning stopped. In Sabrina Peterson's Extra-Fabulous Universe Where Everyone Listened to Her, Saturdays would be zone-out days, when you took all the stuff you didn't get to do during the week and made a delicious ice cream cone out of it, and you ate it all day long. You wouldn't have homework or community service. But you would have ice cream. And hours and hours to mess with your social apps and Infinite Synthesizer, and play music as loud as you liked.

And ice cream, dammit.

>>> <<<

"You know we're going, Sabrina. Stop whining." George meant it.

"But I was gonna work on my virtual band! I got the tracks all lined up, I just need to splice 'em." Sabrina's copper curtain of hair fell over one eye as she hung her head and spoke to the ground. "You never let me do anything."

"So bring that stuff with you. We're going." George touched his earlobe and transmitted, "Chris! Let's go."

"In a minute. Dad, do we have to?"

"Good Lord. Whatever it is you're doing, bring it with you, and let's get to the aircar."

Chris and Sabrina pouted their way out of the pod, both carrying musical instruments with them to pass the time. George figured that whichever bribe worked was fine. Practicing public service was like practicing guitar had been for him as a child—sometimes he didn't want to do it, but eventually he was glad he had. His children might not appreciate it now, but they'd come around.

With the two kids pacified by the Internet and recorded music, the trip to the coast was uneventful. They skimmed over Puget Sound and headed west, over the dark-green fir treetops and snow-dusted peaks of the Olympic Mountains, and on toward the terminus of the coastal road, in casino country. A decades-old U.S. law had first granted gambling licenses to Native tribes here, creating the perfect economic storm, from which the area was still recovering. *Loggers out of work plus the lure of Lady*

Luck, George thought. *Textbook case of income inequality.* Precisely why he'd chosen the site for his community outreach program.

The scattered towns near Kahouk on this remote western tip of Washington state were among the last of the Pacific Ocean settlements to benefit from floating-city technology. While construction at the beachheads further south was underway or completed, the residents here still needed the skills to manage local expansion. Hence, George's pet project—"Tech Soup" kitchens, daylong workshops that brought the latest technology to the people. These took place across the WLC, mainly in rural areas, but wherever limited means left people in need. The Department of Citizen Welfare fully funded the effort, as it addressed several points on the national mission statement at once—and not coincidentally, the two of greatest importance to George Xical and his wife. In order to fulfill their rather more personal mission for a better future, they were eager to make strides toward income and information sharing. George put in the hours one week, and Jennifer the next, usually accompanied by their children.

The soup kitchen shared a site with the local farmers' market, in the huge parking lot of a former Wal-Mart, long since shuttered. The scene was, perhaps, more festive now than it had been then—with stalls of colorful vegetables and flowers, scented soaps and oils, and an electrified bandstand competing for attention. A broad, peaked, rain-repellant covering let in whatever light there might be in mid-February beneath a woolen wrap of clouds, and a system of mirrors and artificial lights enhanced the glow to one worthy of at least an April day. To one side of the fairground, "soup" stations had been set up by more volunteers, with robots, 3-D printers, and augmented-reality spaces where folks could work and play on the latest devices.

A singer's voice drifted over the gathering crowd, and delicious smoke rose from a salmon barbecue. Chris and Sabrina knew better than to try to wheedle their way over to the market side yet. They helped their father unload a box of computer tablets and test the wireless connection, which came and went in this area. Today it was out, so they had to hardwire it. Like magic, a big screen that patched in live video from other soup kitchens came alive with a mass dance demonstration that someone, somewhere, was working on. The camera panned a dense row of downtown buildings and zoomed in on passersby. Guided by biochip technology, hundreds of strangers on the sidewalk suddenly jerked, twirled, and leapt their way in concert, without ever having to learn the steps. Pedestrians young and old, a skateboarder on retro wheels, even a lady in a bionic "walker" skeleton took part. Everything was projected by a hidden server—music, costumes, and obstacles that encouraged some creative acrobatics. Impressive.

"Brin!" George called to his daughter. "Come see this."

It took Sabrina all of thirty seconds to deconstruct the mechanics behind the program. "I could build that," she said, sounding so much like her mother that George did a double take. The girl would be twelve in a few months.

Where would she be in another twenty years? *When I was her age,* George thought, *I was lucky if I could tie my shoes.*

"Maybe you should be broadcasting a demo," George said. "Chris. Why don't you two do a duet? You brought your axes."

This garnered some attention from his children, and occasioned a scenario that George liked to put the two musicians in: jamming together compelled them to adjust their very different playing styles, a form of musical compromise that, he thought, would serve them well in the future. He'd taught Chris the basics of classical guitar himself, which the boy had adapted to current pop styles. Sabrina had started fiddling with computer-synthesized sound as soon as her cognitive skills caught up with her motor skills, at about six years of age. One never knew what she'd come up with on any given day. But, recently, she'd begun writing thematically—a blessing to everyone's ears—and George's heart swelled as he recognized the patterns, bridges, and reprises she embedded in her musical pieces. He couldn't really call them songs, or symphonies. They were more like conversations that perhaps a race of people who spoke through musical notes and percussive beats might conduct.

This development in Brin's grasp of music theory allowed her to play well with others, and had brought her closer to her brother. Chris, who had only tolerated jamming with Sabrina before, now seemed content to follow where her dominant style led. The two liked the idea of beaming a show to the other soup kitchen audiences. They were soon in front of the live Web virtualization cam, making their odd stew of classical electronica for whomever was listening.

George sat back at the check-in desk with a volunteer from the Makah community who acted as a tribal liaison. Greg Renier, known as "Otter" to his friends, had firmly seized on the WLC's outreach offers, hailing them as an honest step up from historically poor relations with the American government. He and the tribal council appreciated the role that technology could play in bumping up the local economy. Each week, Otter rounded up a gaggle of likely suspects and personally escorted them to the fair site, along with their neighbors who sold fish and wild greens at the adjacent market.

Today, three boys near Chris's age abandoned their Net surfing to cluster in front of the square of asphalt that Sabrina had commandeered as a stage.

Otter waved at them and said to George, "They could be brothers, no?"

The Makahs' physical traits echoed many of the Aztecs'—full, straight black hair and dark eyes, thick, resolute mouths set in lovely symmetrical faces, skin a soft shade of brown. All three boys sported hair past their shoulders. More than that, though, the four of them were dressed in cropped pants and water shoes, some wearing long-sleeved T-shirts and some fleece pullovers against the morning chill.

"Hell, they could be a sweet boy band," George teased.

"Led by a sweet girl," Otter flattered George via Sabrina, who had swiftly taken charge of the group as her road crew. She had them stacking produce crates to hold her virtual keyboard and moving a market video banner to form a colorful backdrop for their performance.

George turned his attention to an older white woman who approached the registration table. Her unkempt hair and clothes and a noticeable funk suggested that she was homeless or otherwise extremely down on her luck. George handed her a bottle of liquid nutrition and a few cookies that they kept on hand and asked her how he could help today. She wanted a tutorial on building a sales page into a mobile site for her gleaning business. Nomadic by choice, she followed the seasons to gather wild mushrooms, fern fiddleheads, cedar bark, and mistletoe to sell.

"I'll take this one," Otter said, ushering her to the next worktable, where he could coach her on setting up computer forms and locating free payment platforms.

Watching them work, satisfaction settled like a mantle on George's shoulders. This was precisely the reason for the tech soup kitchens—to equalize the opportunities that added quality to life. He watched the woman listen intently to Otter and then ask him detailed questions, even taking over the keypad to show him a thing or two. The income she would get, George knew, depended directly upon the woman's grasp of the technology she needed to reach her market.

He felt the gentle nudge of humility knocking on his psyche, and Jennifer, the voice of his conscience in that department, came to mind. *I know, dear: you told me so. You were right.* He hadn't always given information science— his wife's passion—the regard it deserved.

>>> <<<

It was the third week of the worst month of their lives. George and Jennifer, and the rest of western North America, had awakened three weeks earlier to urgent phone calls from the east: "Turn on the news. Quick!"

George had fumbled with his notebook computer, which insisted on running an update before opening its Web browser. He swore, "*¡Que se joda y se rompa ahorita!*"—then quickly amended his call for the laptop to fuck and destroy itself—"em, I mean, as soon as I'm done with you...."

His aggravation was erased by the scenes that flashed across his screen: a series of fiery explosions, each one spinning a smoke plume into the air, and a subsequent stampede of people—brown people—half-dressed, some dragging children by the hand, some carrying infants, all eyes reflecting panic. *What's going on?*

"Holy fucking shit!"

The baby started crying in the next room, and Jennifer rolled out of bed and headed for the door.

"Jen!" George called her back, his voice sounding urgent enough to stop her in her tracks. "*¡Míralo!*" He thrust the screen at her. "Look!"

The volume was too low to hear. She read the feed, half to herself: "... 'moments ago, declaration of war coming after the first strikes made on Nueva Laredo'—What? By who?"

Sabrina's cries grew into shrieks, now easily dismissed in favor of the news onscreen.

"It's Grubb!" George shouted, pulling on his pants. "He's—he's bombed the border!"

Jennifer jammed the volume key higher. The female commentator's tone was nearly as frantic as George's. "… repeat, U.S. has declared war on Mexico, engaging in simultaneous strikes at key cities on its northern border. Confirmed so far are bombings at Tijuana, Ciudad Juarez, and Nueva Laredo…."

"It's a wall of bombs," Jennifer whispered, which George barely registered as he instructed his phone to "call Mom." He immediately got a cut-off signal.

"Shit. Shit!"

Jennifer reached out and grasped his hand, pulling him back to the bed, where she sat with her eyes glued to the laptop screen. "Shh," she said. "They'll be fine. They're nowhere near the border." This was meant less to soothe him than to lay another brick to the small foundation of what they knew to be happening.

"The port cities will be next," he predicted tersely, focusing on the screen with her and ignoring their child's wild cries.

"Dad? Mom?" Four-year-old Chris had wandered into the room, wearing pajama bottoms, the remnants of sleep in his eyes.

George had mechanically drawn him close. "Shush!" he ordered as the newswoman jerkily conveyed the information coming from her earpiece, one hand to the device as if to wring good news from it.

Both he and Jennifer were right, at least on that day. George's family—his *mamá*, his *papá*, and grandmother,

Abuela Santa—were not harmed in those first chaotic attacks on three Mexican cities, just south of the American border. As President Grubb often did following an attack, he immediately offered a truce. President Cenobio had no choice but to accept the terms—a cessation in all trade between Mexico and the U.S., pending treaty renegotiations.

George remembered that reprieve as a time of renewed hope, in the face of the U.S. leader's hopelessly cruel choice of targets.

The first communities harmed—Nuevo Laredo and the rest—were border towns of modest size, whose inhabitants had been painted more broadly with brush strokes of poverty than the thin lines of subversion, of which President Grubb had accused them. Besides smacking down the drug trade, his stated justification for war was a trade imbalance instigated, he claimed, by the local hard-working farm, sweatshop, and factory laborers. The more plausible truth was that, unable to secure funds for a physical barrier, he had used the military's ready budget to build a wall of bombs, as Jennifer had called it.

World condemnation, as well as aid donations, came quickly. Medical help poured into the border towns from Cuba, Spain, and Canada, followed by courageous envoys of humanitarian groups from San Diego and Los Angeles. CALIFORNIA DEFIES U.S. GOVERNMENT TO INTERVENE IN WAR ON MEXICO, read the headlines, and with the truce, George had relaxed ever so slightly. He abandoned his new job in the state capital to hole up with his brothers, Gary, Gaban, and Gilberto, at the family's business headquarters.

From Monterey, they followed the unfolding events in their homeland with cautious optimism.

But the port cities were targeted next, two weeks later. This time, the Pentagon blindsided Mexico's major air force bases. Revelations that the truce was a hoax came not from news outlets or even the warning signs and sounds of an invasion, but from a simple shout-out on the Internet. The American leader trampled on the white flag and jeered at his targets, outright announcing the armed forces' next moves:

@officialHaroldGrubb How stupid is Mexico not two know it's coast is now as defenceless as open northern border, shd have paid for wall when u had the chance!

Up in Monterey, in the executive office littered with takeout wrappers and coffee cups, Gilberto read this feed aloud to his brothers as the news channels confirmed three simultaneous strikes, in Veracruz, Ensenada—and La Paz. The four of them watched the live newscast in horror, instantly recognizing the waterfront Malecon Road in their ancestral home, a sudden hell on earth amid the pouring smoke and flames rising where gas mains had been hit.

In the days that followed, they heard no reports of family members, dead or alive. The Xical men, all born in the United States and all given to action, quickly divvied up their loyalties. The two youngest, Gary and Gaban, joined a junta group that was sending manpower south from every major California city, as reinforcements, if ground troops were called in. They'd be able to get information about loved ones and what resources the military needed, and where. George and Gilberto, both employed by the state, decided to remain and muster what help they could from Sacramento.

Jennifer had completed her doctorate, and George had moved her and the kids to the state capital, where he'd been hired as an assistant economic advisor to the governor. Gilberto had taken over administrative duties for Xical Ltd., the family shipping business, when their father, Gonzalo, had retired and moved back to La Paz. Uncertainty and crisis now cut ugly detours through the placid course that they'd envisioned for the future.

True to his style of overkill, Grubb's military leaders hit their foes hard, again targeting the same six ports and border towns that had already taken the most fatal of blows. These offensives were foreshadowed—if one read between the lines—by abusive Internet salvos. Given the president's habit of broadcasting nonsense, these text messages fell on blind eyes, to be resurrected as missed warnings later.

In the surreal days that followed, Jennifer gave George every rock she had to lean on. Even after they learned the names of the dead and came to grips with missed funerals and irrevocable loss, she steadied him. When Mexico eventually turned the tables and prevailed, she helped him find something to celebrate. But in the aftermath and finger pointing that sought to lay blame and prevent a reoccurrence, two things happened that would forever change George's outlook.

First, his resident state of California voted for and declared secession from the United States and alliance with Mexico. Second, Jennifer pointed out that if every Mexican citizen had had access to the Internet, much loss of life could have been prevented. It was the sort of hindsight that may or may not have been borne out in truth. But it was a possibility, George had to admit.

As the wounds scarred up, reopened, and were covered over again by time and the love of his family, George returned to his work with new fervor. It wasn't enough to throw money at problems, to shore up the poor folks of Nuevo Laredo or Tijuana, or even those of Stockton and Fresno. Numbers wouldn't help them get ahead, for money burned faster than the paper on which it was printed. They needed more than money. They needed the means to rebuild.

One evening, as George ranted about construction brigades and training credits as cures for the have-nots, Jennifer took him aside. She quieted him and sat him down with Sabrina, who had just turned two. The child was playing with an old touchscreen phone. Jennifer stood back as George watched their daughter, without prompting, open a games folder. Little Sabrina studied the balls of color spat onto the tiny screen by a random-pattern generator. For every equation she finished, she earned a flashing light and a burble of sound, causing her to coo with delight.

"Let it be a lesson, Xical," Jennifer gently chided her husband. "People don't need handouts. They need tools. They need the most powerful tool we can give them."

George opened his mouth to argue, but another glance at Sabrina showed him what Jennifer meant. She'd been saying it all along, with her life's work, but he hadn't heard her clearly, until now. It was access to information that would put people on equal footing, that would let them march ahead and traverse borders. High-tech, low-tech… the form didn't matter so much as the result.

"Don't you see?" Jennifer took George by the hand. "If information was free for the taking, money would lose its value."

George gaped at her. The concept alone was dangerous, reckless—and spot on.

Cash had finite value. Information, though, was the tool that could build every other tool.

>>> <<<

"Okay, kids, let's go," George said, after their three-hour soup kitchen shift came to a close.

They'd been so engrossed in their new musical game with their new friends that they hadn't once asked to go buy kettle corn or even go to the bathroom.

"Just a few more minutes." Chris huddled with one of the boys over the sound box of his guitar. The youngster appeared to be interested in building instruments.

Sabrina ignored the signal to leave, hiding behind her green barricade of hair as she pursued the electronic riff she was composing.

George, ready to pack up, grew impatient with the routine disobedience. "Now!" he thundered.

Sabrina merely raised her head and met his snapping eyes. "Da-ad," she drawled. "I thought you wanted us to *participate.*"

Damn. She was right.

CHAPTER 9

James Ting ran a tight district department, known among the WLC administration for its high security, low overhead, and no bullshit. How he did this with consistency was a matter of conjecture. His children, now grown, had once believed he had eyes in the back of his head—and, perhaps, they still did. His employees also thought his success hinged on physical, rather than intellectual, superiority. Many of them characterized his butt cheeks as being so rigid that he could insert a pole between them and write his name in hardening concrete with perfect penmanship. The truth, Jennifer thought, lay somewhere in between.

The tight-asshole theory could have been a misperception based on Ting's spring-loaded posture. His perfect carriage came from daily tai chi practice, which made him more, not less flexible, in both mind and body. And the reaches of his intellect, Jennifer thought, were distant, and difficult to see.

She regarded him now from her seat, at a right angle to his, at one end of the modest boardroom desk. James Ting had only an inch or two of height on Jennifer, and shaggy hair to his chin, much like hers but for the fading black color that showed a few stray gray hairs. If not for those telltales, his age might have been anywhere upward of twenty-seven, twenty-eight, or so. His ruddy-tan complexion was free of wrinkles, and the brows above his brown eyes were jet black. Hands as smooth as any lab geek's rested on the wide desk. His voice was clear and strong as he briefed Jennifer on the reason for their meeting.

"Leaks," he said, sounding more resigned than alarmed.

Jennifer took this as a sign that their department database was not the one sprouting holes. "Who's getting hit?" she asked.

"Applications." He activated the desk hologram and read off the text's main points: "'Outgoing departmental decisions to local hubs—Housing, Transportation, Education.'" Graphs of their budget figures appeared beneath each heading. Below those were examples of the most recent ethics decisions that guided those budgets. The money came from taxes and other revenue, and would be doled out according to the grade issued to each proposition by the ethics department.

"Housing, transportation, and education," Jennifer murmured. She knew their fiscal and national security ratings. "Those are big, but they're not that big. I mean, there's a lot of money moving through them, but the district departments don't handle matters of Core safety. Who do you think wants their intel?"

Ting nudged the desk interface, and the next frame appeared.

"DDCI! That's Ameristates."

The graphic annotation read: DEPARTMENT OF DE CENTRALIZED INTELLIGENCE, with arrows connected to WALL STREET, HUMAN RESOURCES, and FOREIGN IMPORTS.

"I don't get it." Jennifer said. "Why specifically ethics-based initiatives?"

"Ethics, they don't care about." Ting turned to the next frame and let her read it.

An enlarged scan of an old print memo showed a directive from the Whitehouse™, stamped CLASSIFIED. It was dated January 5, 2021, soon after four states had joined California to form the Western Land Core. The opening paragraph laid out an espionage plan to track how the collective spent its money internally—the budget procedure used, its allotments, and any foreign deals that might be made to achieve its goals.

"But this plan is nearly ten years old," Jennifer said.

"As we know, the Grubb administration is not... real swift," Ting pointed out. "They found out that moving too fast only slowed down their progress. I hear they're still using print documents because they think they're less vulnerable to interception than digital transmissions."

Jennifer was baffled by the targets of their data mining. "But, wouldn't they have gotten all this stuff by now?"

"This is the first known instance that they've penetrated our firewalls. Like I said"—Ting gave a wide smile that showed brown, tea-stained teeth—"they're not real swift. Grubb the First talked tough on 'the cyber' but couldn't use a computer."

"And you think Grubb 2.0 might make some headway?"

He nodded. "This came down from Mountain View. The op in question looks to be a smokescreen for the Big One."

Jennifer's eyes went wide. "Whoa."

The WLC's national intelligence labs clustered in Mountain View, the California location of the West's most influential technological research firms. The latter's trade secrets and the former's heavy security detail made the Bay Area nexus the logical site for the nation's highest priority initiatives. These largely had to do with clean energy, military hardware, medical advancement—and robotics.

Ting gestured at this list on the screen. "We believe one or all of these represent the real target. Ameristates has fallen behind in the research. Our IT products would be extremely valuable to them. And both Grubbs have been known to take without giving, while posing as deal makers."

Jennifer sat up straighter. Her mind whirled with questions.

Which one of those things was the Big One? Who knew what Grubb's priorities were? Could his spies have learned of a connection to Jennifer's work through their routine sifting through the applications department files?

Jennifer said cautiously, "My bet is on medical intel. Old Man Grubb is hanging on by an eyelash. They need what we've got to keep him alive."

"Or extend his life," Ting added.

What had become routine surgery and replacement in the West was unavailable to Ameristates citizens, thanks to the sanctions against the WLC that had never been lifted. This had caused Jennifer much anxiety in recent years, as her parents aged and the freedom to emigrate was denied them. Grubb the Second had only further isolated his country and could no longer reach out to the European and Asian nations that had also forged ahead in bioengineering and medical nanotechnology.

While this observation might partially explain the espionage, it didn't address who in the applications department might be complicit in releasing information. It also didn't give voice to Jennifer's stronger sentiment—that the States would likely want to be the first to acquire artificial consciousness technology. An army of thinking robots would do much to blast them out of the international pit they'd dug for themselves.

"So, James. Are you implying that we've got a mole in the department? Or one in Applications?"

Ting shut down the holographic display. "We don't know what we don't know yet. I'm briefing on a need-to-know basis, one on one. That way, if anyone blows a hole in our shields, I'll know who to talk to. But we'll be locking down our file sharing with Applications. Also keeping a complete inventory of both data shares and lab hardware." He raised his eyebrows at Jennifer. "And I'll be watching."

"Yes, sir." Jennifer cringed. What else did he know?

"I mean it. I'll tolerate no slip-ups from Ethics. As they say, 'a straight foot is not afraid of a crooked shoe.'"

She forced a cool assurance. "My feet will be as straight as they come, James."

He eyed her, smiling his incongruously threatening smile—the one that showed no teeth. "They'd better be."

>>> <<<

Jennifer retrieved Maxi from the locked lab, her eyes drifting to the supply cupboard and back to the dog's eyes. Sabrina had been upset to find that Maxi's security implant, like hers and her brother's, had shaded their pet's blue eyes gray. Brin complained and asked if they could order a new color scheme. Jennifer, already wound tightly over the Maxi issue, denied the request. When asked why, she'd added, "Because I said so!"

She'd had her reasons. And Ting had his for playing the authoritarian, no matter what the underlings said about him. He did his best to keep the lab secure and admin off their backs.

Jennifer wondered if the time would ever come when she could approach the honchos at Mountain View and let them in on her progress—or collaborate with them. Every workday, she diverted the finished reviews to Val2001's drive, and every night, she moved the material to Maxi's for safekeeping. In this manner, she inched toward the day—hour, second, instant—when she would direct Val/Maxi to perform the function, whatever it was, that ignited a separate awareness. How close to this were the national researchers? How close were Grubb's people to finding out?

Jennifer sighed, steeling herself to more waiting and more secrecy. If the big boys and babes at national security were anticipating trouble, there wasn't much point in connecting with them before her big bang actually happened.

If it happened.

When.

Jennifer nervously transferred Val's latest files for the trip home. "There ya go, sweet pea," she said, chucking Maxi under the chin. Then she synced the dog to her bracelet and, already violating the new departmental inventory rule, left the lab.

>>> <<<

Maxi lay under a rhododendron bush on the sidelines of a red-clay court while Jennifer and George played a game of tennis. The dog's collar flashed red and blue, a sign that she was alert and watching her keepers intently.

"Fifteen-forty," Jennifer called as the turquoise ball retrieved itself to her hand. She bounced it a few times and then served. The ball narrowly caught the baseline on George's side of the court and skipped past his reach.

"Tsch," George chided himself.

"Thirty-forty." She repeated the play, correctly assuming that he wouldn't expect lightning to strike twice in the same place.

"Deuce!" he scored for her, and jumped in place a bit, legs spread, to focus himself. "Come on, mama. Bring it on."

Jennifer tried a third time but could not place the ball as precisely, and George let it pass. She frowned. "Outside."

Her next short serve was returned handily by George from the forecourt. She popped it up, and they rallied across the net twice more, each, before George lobbed the ball over her head. It hit at the service line and skipped out of bounds.

George's next serve was strong, and Jennifer missed the ball to hand him the game and set. Maxi whined beneath her shrub. George did a mock winner's dance and let out a loud breath, mimicking the roar of a crowd.

"I quit," Jennifer pouted, heading for the towels and water they'd left on a bench near Maxi. The dog whined again, and Jennifer patted her. "She thinks you cheated, George."

"She thinks the sun rises out of your asshole," he tossed back, approaching them. "That mutt's loyalty knows no bounds. Just like your serves," he quipped. "Good set," he added more sincerely, toweling off a sweaty arm. He switched the blue tennis ball to manual mode and tossed it for Maxi to fetch.

They both watched as the dog grabbed it in her mouth, and then did something strange. She hopped up and down on all fours, then bounced the ball off the ground and caught it in her teeth a few times. Then Maxi turned her head and whipped the tennis ball at Jennifer, who braced a hand and caught it on reflex.

She turned to George. "Did you see that? Since when does she volley and throw? It's as if she picked it up from us, just now."

"Right. She'll be the next Wimbledon champ," he joked.

The spring day had beckoned OC-3 residents to the park that lay dead-center among the city's pedways and buildings, with air temperature just 70 degrees and enough sunshine to throw shadows. A broad, open lawn formed a quilt of activity—a pair of teenagers playing Frisbee, scattered singles reading or snacking, a dozen Muslims practicing *salat* on colorful rugs.

Jennifer noted the contrast between that prayer group and another collection of faithfuls singing a Hindu chant, not far off. "Everyone thinks their beliefs are the most 'right,'" she grumbled.

"Hey," George countered, "spirit is spirit. As long as it's used in the spirit for which it was intended. As my *papá* used to announce when he'd smoosh his rice and beans and meat together: 'is all going to the same place.'"

This drew a chuckle, and silent assent. They rested a few more minutes until a group of doubles came to play. George and Jennifer relinquished the court and moved off down the cushioned path with their pet.

A blaze of yellow caught Jennifer's eye as a goldfinch streaked by. Maxi saw it, too. She barked and chased it a bit, dutifully returning to Jennifer's side and trotting after her. They passed a couple of twenty-something guys on the grass, whose loud talk tapered into veiled appreciative stares that George pretended not to notice.

Even in a sweat-darkened shirt, his wife turned heads. "So, what's the latest on Leakgate?" George asked. "Are your feet still straight?"

Jennifer returned his grin and kicked out with a tennis shoe. "No hammer toes or bunions here. C'mon. Let's sit down." She led him to another bench near a graceful rocklike bridge that sent the path over a small fountain. A horse and rider drew near, and Jennifer warned her pet to stay close. "Maxi, no." The dog kept its gray eyes on the pair but lay down at her mistress's feet.

"Ting is on the warpath," Jennifer then replied. "I'm starting to freak about the daily data dump. Sooner or later, he's bound to suspect something's up with Maxi. I wish I could just continue working with her from home, but I don't want to get into a long-distance transfer if there's a possibility of an intercept."

"I hear you. Just be careful," George said. "You get canned, and it all goes up in smoke." He reached down and stroked the dog's back. "I believe in you, Jen. What you're doing—it could make all the difference. For our kids, their kids…."

"Back at you, love-man." Jennifer ran a hand through her short, damp hair, raising it into spikes. "You're the one opening it all up to everyone else's kids."

They were quiet long enough for a house sparrow to run through its song. Jennifer caught the edge of George's sleeve and pointed out the round, red-tinged female bird on a low-hanging tree branch.

"When are you leaving for Sequoia?" she asked him, meaning the WLC capital city, which adjoined Mountain View and floated in San Francisco Bay.

"Two weeks. We're doing at least five days of hearings," George said. His office was presenting key legislation that would make public any further advances in additive manufacturing—yet another controversial move in the effort toward equitable resource allocation. The arguments against it were coming, as expected, from the very wealthy and the very poor subsets, or as George dubbed them, the willfully selfish and the selflessly willful. The first group was fighting tooth and nail to hang onto what they had and could get, while the second found no gain in larger numbers joining their group. These skeptics saw only a lose-lose situation in which the rich would gobble up even more of their share. The harder George's colleagues tried to convince them otherwise, the deeper they dug in their heels.

"Well, *you* be careful," Jennifer said, snuggling her warm shoulder against his. "The kids need you. The Rendezvous campout is coming up, and after that, Chris has Battle of the Bands."

"Hey, I'll take the virtual battles over the real ones anytime." George threw her a glance. "Remember when those kids worked him over last year? Who saw that coming?" Some teenagers had roughed up Chris and his fencing partner in the park one day. George wanted to intervene with their parents, but his wife persuaded him to let Chris handle it on his own.

Jennifer shook her head, anger over the incident returning. "Yes, he's slender. Yes, he's prettier than some girls. So he likes to dress up in costumes and play with swords. So, what? A certain type of kid is threatened by that kind of creativity," she muttered. "Some things never change."

"Oh, yeah?" George gave her a long look. "What about your dad?" He patted Jennifer's knees, calling Maxi up to balance on hind legs and perch against them. "Somebody once told me that information is a tool for change. You think people are trapped by ignorance? Then, you change 'em, Jen." He thumped the dog's side. "You change 'em."

CHAPTER 10

Chris Xical lay hidden in a screen of brush, trying not to make a sound. He'd never realized how hard this was to do. Just breathing rocked his body enough to broadcast the deafening crunch of dry grass and the rustle of his calico shirt. Surely any intruder would hear the noise and come after him.

He tried holding his breath.

Fifteen seconds of this told him he'd have to either risk some noise or show himself. Slowly, carefully, he exhaled, willing himself to relax into jelly. Just then, a louder sound signaled movement nearby. Chris tensed. Through the leaves, he saw something brown pass by, then hesitate. Was it a man, or beast?

He prepared himself for the unknown.

"Yahh-ahhh!" Chris yelled, jumping up and lunging toward the trespasser.

As he sprang from cover, he saw that he faced two opponents—but one was battling the other, and neither had noticed the young mountaineer. Chris stared at the huge rear end of a grizzly bear. The great animal raised itself on two legs and swiped at the Indian girl who cowered below, doing nothing else to transmit her fear.

Shakily, Chris raised his Colt revolver and cocked the hammer with his thumb. But the heavy firearm slipped from his grasp and fell to the ground, discharging smoke and a harmless shot. His only thought was to save the girl. He pulled a throwing knife from his waist and instinctively slung it toward the bear's side. The animal gave a half-growl and a cough, and fell to the ground.

Chris pushed forward. "Are you al—" In the same instant, he saw a tomahawk lodged in the bear's throat, which poured blood, and felt a blow to his own neck.

"You died!" came the referee's voice as Chris stumbled the ground, chagrinned. Then he flooded with relief at having made it through the exercise.

Chris and his club mate, Anna, got to their feet and made their way to the judging box. His virtual pistol and throwing knife and her tomahawks, as well as the dead bear, had frizzled away to nothing as the game ended. They both wore buckskin—Chris a pair of rough pants and moccasins, and Anna a fringed dress—appropriately clothing them for the mid 1800s.

Chris pulled on the wide brim of his felt hat and nodded at Anna. "Good match," he acknowledged.

"Good try," she said graciously.

Once the scoring was done, Chris found he'd racked up a few points: two for quick action, two for bravery, and two for his moral choice to kill the bear first, not his opponent. These last two were overturned, however, because the choice had cost him his life, and his rival had conquered him.

Sabrina had been watching the scenario and caught up with Chris. Her athletic shorts and shirt set off his period costume among the swirl of festival-goers on the grassy expanse. "Way to go, bro," she said facetiously, although she'd been impressed. "Beat by a girl."

Chris socked her in the arm, none too gently. He didn't need the reminder. And he realized that if he'd been up against his sister, he probably still would've lost. "Can I help it if I'm wired to save damsels in distress?" he stuck up for himself.

"It looked like Anna Two Tomahawks was doing just fine without you." Sabrina softened. "But that must've been scary! That bear sure looked real."

Chris appreciated the concession. "It smelled real too. But it was worth it. Look what I won." He grinned and opened his palm to reveal a bear claw replica.

"Noble."

"Wait'll I show Dad. He's gonna be my dueling partner in the throwing contest."

"Nice of the league leaders to let the parents play, huh? Are you going to let him win?" she teased, linking arms with him.

Chris pushed his hat back on his head. "I might have to do that. Come watch us." Sabrina had a singular charm that could erase any slight, and there were usually plenty of those to overcome. "So, what's next for you, little sister?"

She waved at a row of sun-shaded booths to one side of the demonstration area. "First, I'm gonna hit Mom's concession and get some chocolate lemonade, for energy.

Then I'm doing dog agility with Mena's border collie. Me and Bam-Bam have been practicing for, like, a month."

Chris knew that Jennifer had nixed the idea of competing with Maxi—something about too much wear on her pistons, or something. It wasn't as though pistons were irreplaceable. He thought his mother was being overprotective. Sabrina thought she was being a butthead. "Well, good luck," Chris said to his sister. "D'you think you'll earn your Keepers badge?"

She brushed a slice of royal-blue hair behind an ear. "Of course." Spying somebody coming their way, Sabrina leaned into Chris with her tucked arm and steered him in the other direction. "Don't look now, but here comes trouble."

Chris glanced over his shoulder, slowing the pace. "I said don't—"

"*Hi*, mountain man," came a female voice, and Chris felt his arm being removed from his sister's embrace. He turned to find a teenage girl with long, curly blonde hair and highly developed body curves doing something crazy with her eyelashes in his direction.

"Glynna. What do you want?" Sabrina said coldly, before Chris had a chance reply.

The girl ignored her. "I like your hat," she purred, plucking the field hat from Chris's head and placing it on hers.

"I made it myself, with my clan," Chris said, taking the compliment literally and not for the come-on it was. "I printed the felt, and then we all shaped and embellished 'em to get our Trappers badge." He went on to describe how he'd made his reed hatband.

Glynna wasn't listening to the process. "Could you make me one like yours?"

"Well, sure...." He didn't see his sister roll her eyes.

Sabrina edged a shoulder between them and inserted herself there. "I didn't know you were in Quest, Glynna. You're not in Buckskinners or Ambassadors. Are you a Cosmonaut?"

This caused a torrent of derisive giggles.

"What's so funny?" Sabrina snapped.

"That's so little-kid," the older girl said, and Chris ducked his head to hide his embarrassment. "Nah," Glynna went on, "my brother's in the league; he's working on his Stargazer. I'm just here for the refreshments. And the hats," she added, suddenly whirling and running off.

"Hey!" Chris started after her, then stopped, eyeing his sister.

"Don't—" Sabrina watched Glynna run off and gave up. She threw her hands in the air. "Oh, go on. Go on."

>>> <<<

George stood watching the Mountaineers' trials from a distance. Jen was right; at fourteen, it was time for Chris to strike out on his own. Hell, it was probably past time, but a certain amount of human loss left a guy spooky.

The physical wrenching that attended thoughts of his family's deaths triggered him to shut his eyes and call up his meditation scene: a protective cove of green-blue sea, with dark, rocky cliffs bowing to soft, gray sands, and the white spray of breakers fading into the shallows. He let his mind go silent, and he counted backward from ten, his head dipping slightly with each beat. Then he opened his eyes.

Positive thoughts, Xical. The Rendezvous camp scene reminded him of one from his past, when he was a boy, a bit younger than Chris. He'd been hiking in the canyons east of Monterey, on a day meant to test his skills with a map and compass. His father, Juan, had always sought to equip his sons with the means to navigate on land and sea. So, Gilberto, the eldest, had learned the intricacies of the outlying hills and valleys from Juan, and he'd passed his knowledge on to George, in weekend treks through chaparral country.

Today was George's turn to demonstrate his facility by leading his brothers through the orienteering trial sponsored by local law enforcement. Gary, eleven, and Gaban, ten, had been introduced to the region on hikes but had never had to make time, as they would today. There would be no control points or contact with event officials along the way, just an all-out push to the final destination.

A couple dozen enthusiasts knotted around the Start flag, in a scrub-dotted flatland shouldered by gently rolling hills. Juan stood with his boys, taking in the lay of the land but not offering any direction. The course was open, leaving the route up to the leader. George studied the paper map. After some deliberation, he chose to avoid a climb and take a low trajectory, which would drop them deep into an arroyo that would spit them out very near the mouth of the stream that marked the finish line.

A mix of pride and anxiety filled George as the three boys sprinted away from the starting point. They raced across the open expanse peppered with chaparral, toward a wooded canyon, in which they were soon enveloped. Wide competitor intervals left them in solitude, and they slowed to a rapid walk beneath the mix of towering redwood trees, riparian shrubbery, and low-growing ground cover.

The March day was chilly, and the fog that sifted through the arroyo left a sheen of damp on every leaf and rock. Slick ground that would be dry and dusty in just a few weeks offered little traction underfoot. As they struck off on a narrow deer path, the two younger boys' excitement led to a shoving match to see who would go first in line.

"I'm older," Gary argued.

"Yeah, but maybe I'm faster," Gaban suggested, sliding a bit as he tried to prove it.

"Careful, guys," young George warned his brothers. "If you fall and get hurt, there's no one to call for help. It'll be a long way out of here." George solved the dispute by putting Gary in the lead, Gaban second, and bringing up the rear himself, so he could keep an eye on them both.

After a time, consultation between compass and map brought them within sound range of the creek that George was looking for. It was all downhill from there. The rush of water over rocks falsely promised a much larger water body than they encountered, which was good, because they'd have to cross it.

"Keep your eyes peeled for a likely spot, *hermanitos*," he tasked his brothers, to further their education.

Gary spotted a flat log that spanned the rocky brook and acted as a natural foot bridge.

"Good job, Gare," George said. He noticed Gaban's shoulders droop; competition defined the relationship between the two, so close in age. So George pointed to a clump of greenery that sprouted white flowers at their feet and asked, "Which of you can tell me what that plant is?"

"I know!" Gaban shot back. "It's poison oak."

Gary sulked a bit. "Why don't you pick some, then?"

The trio pressed steadily on, jogging when the trail flattened out and slowing to steer around roots, fallen logs, and errant vines in their way. In this manner, nearly two hours flew by. At last, George noticed his brothers begin to flag. According to his map, they were about forty-five minutes or so from the Finish. "Not far now!" he encouraged them.

No sooner had he said this than Gaban stumbled and lost his balance. As if in slow motion, the boy slid on a muddy downslope, hands first, and gave a few short cries. Then he fell beneath the shrub line and was lost to George's view.

Gary had doubled back, and George hustled forward, yelling, "Gaban! Gaban!" They both peered over the brush to spy their brother at the bottom of a muddy ravine. He was moving, then he pushed to his hands and knees—then fell back to the ground.

"Gaban!" Gary called. "Are you alright?"

The boy's reply was muffled, but he stirred again.

George cautioned, "Don't try to move! We're coming!"

This was easier said than done. There appeared to be two options: go down the way Gaban had, hands first, or slide down on their bottoms. Either way was going to hurt. Gary and George slid-inched their way toward their brother, feet first, mud piling up on their hiking shoes and fingers as they grasped at underbrush for handholds. Gaban's form appeared larger and larger, until finally, George was upon him. The boy had ignored his counsel and was sitting upright, patting his arms.

The sleeves of his dark-blue shirt had ripped nearly all the way off, showing dirt streaks and raw skin. George carefully looked his brother over, checking his eyes for signs of concussion and pressing on arms and legs to search for bone breaks. Satisfied, he and Gary helped Gaban gingerly to his feet and let him get his bearings. Then George realized he'd better check his own. He pulled out the map and compass, which he'd secured in a closed pocket.

As he took a reading, Gary looked over his shoulder at the steep drop-off they'd just traversed. "Holy crap! We'll never get back up this thing. How do we know where we are, George?" Without waiting for an answer, he accused Gaban, "We told you to watch where you're going. You've wrecked our chances!"

"I—I'm sorry," Gaban choked, sounding as though he were about to cry.

George raised his gaze from the map. Gary, who acted tough, was tired, and more afraid than he would let on. Gaban had simply taken a wrong step. "Hey!" George cut in. "Could've happened to anybody," he said, putting his arm around his youngest sibling. "Gare—c'mere. Check this out."

He spread out the map and stabbed a finger at it. "We're here. And the finish line, as near as I can tell, is… here."

He paused, and the three exchanged glances.

Gary's expression softened. "But… that's *close*."

A grin spread across George's muddy face. "Damn straight. Closer than it would've been going the other way!" He squeezed Gaban's shoulder, and the boy sniffed away tears.

They marched toward the sound of trickling water once more, out of the ravine, and across a sand beach to the finish line, where their father waited. By this time, muddy and bruised though he was, Gaban's energy had risen with the dramatic turn their adventure had taken. "Pa!" he called. "Guess what! I found us a shortcut!"

A light breeze cooled George's perspiring forehead, and he refocused on the present, feeling the echoing pang of loss. But that had been a good day, one of teaching and learning. And loving. How he missed them.

Again, at the sad sensation, he made himself look ahead, look forward. The Buckskinner trial had ended, and folks had moved off to picnic or take in other events. Recorded music played from a distant speaker. There, on the lawn, was his son, Chris—hatless, black hair streaking behind him, running awkwardly in his moccasins after a young girl.

Fourteen. He pressed his lips together in a slight smile. *Jen's always right.*

>>> <<<

Jennifer sat with George and Philomena under a canopy at the lemonade booth, which had been erected near the animal trials arena. The "Keepers," as the club pet handlers were called, would demonstrate the skills they'd been honing in order to earn their leadership badges. Again Maxi and Bam-Bam, the two robotic herding dogs, attended their mistresses, play-tussling in between naps.

Philomena, dressed sharply as always in a paisley dress and several scarves, took a sip of her drink and smacked her lips. "Gawd," she said to her friends. "Who'da thunk chocolate was so damn good in lemonade?"

George grinned. "It was Jen's idea."

Jennifer spread her hands. "Hey, I was just joking when I said it. Then Brin had the bot mix some up, and, well, the rest is history." She paused. "At least, it will be when I wash this stuff off. I'm sticky all over from serving."

Sabrina came running up to the booth, her blue hair flying away from her face, which showed animation today instead of her usual cynical demeanor. "Mom! Mom! Emergency lemonade request. I'm up in twenty minutes."

Jennifer smiled to herself. Her daughter was learning to manage her time. She'd have to remember to tell George that she'd told him so; he'd balked over the decision to let the kids to opt out of community service so they could join the Quest League. After all, they had paid their dues at the tech soup kitchen for a long time.

Hers had been the least of the lobbying efforts. Chris was mad to get into the club. "Please, Dad," he'd begged.

"Roger Cho is one of Buckskinners, and he gets to build fires and shoot muzzleloaders and go on camping trips. That's, like, my dream!"

"I thought sword fighting was your thing," George had said drolly.

Chris scoffed, "That was last year. Buckskinners learn how to use real stuff like they had back in mountain-man times. They mess around with skins and pelts, and there's wild-animal attacks—"

"What?"

"Well, they're virtual, Dad. Nobody gets hurt."

"But everybody has *fun*," his sister, Sabrina, put in. She, too, was ready to trade Saturday service days for club meetings and campouts. "You know, fun? It should be in the parent's dictionary, under things you gave up a long time ago."

At this comment, Jennifer had caught George's eye and suppressed a smirk. Rather than be shown up as a fuddy-duddy, he had acquiesced. Later, Jennifer tried to make him feel good about the decision. "You've said yourself that Quest League is good for kids," she reminded him. "And they do a lot of what gets done at the soup kitchens—there are citizenship badges, and all kinds of things to build skills and self-reliance."

"Like playing with virtual weaponry," he'd said with sarcasm.

"Which boys do anyway. Might as well give them some structure," she argued.

Structure, they'd received, and George and Jennifer got a good dose of it too. Quest parents were expected to head meetings and chaperone outings, all of which led to the big annual blow-out, Rendezvous. Even Sabrina gushed about the area-wide gathering, in which the club's members moved up in the ranks. This had pushed George over the edge. Anything that positively motivated his daughter was worth a try. So the two children had thrown themselves into the club's events, and their parents had enjoyed the dividends.

Jennifer took a token from Sabrina and let her daughter serve herself from the drink machine as the dog agility class was announced. The trial was about to start.

Chris, who had retrieved his hat, wandered over at the last moment.

"Where've you been?" asked George.

The boy opened his mouth, but Sabrina preempted him again. "Chris has a girlfriend."

"Do not!" Chris slumped to the ground in huff.

Philomena tossed Jennifer a glance. "Ssh! They're starting. Brin?" Mena offered her a vacant chair, but the girl was too wound up to sit down.

Her agitation woke Maxi, who had been resting. "Come on, girl," Sabrina said, crouching next to the dog. "Let's watch the first two go. Then me and Bam-Bam have to warm up."

The dog agility trial was no virtual game; the obstacles and participants were very real. In fact, both biological and robotic animals would compete over the same course, with appropriate scoring adjustments made for speed and difficulty. This circumstance spoke to the inclusive nature of the club and the Rendezvous: young people from all over Washington state experienced each other's local color. Folks outside the smartcities tended to keep live animals at home, while those with greater access to technology and who were bound by clean-air laws made do with robotic pets. These were now so sophisticated that, in some ways, they exceeded the traits that people loved about real animals.

Jennifer watched Maxi give Sabrina a lick with her bioengineered tongue and turned her attention to the arena. The grass square was surrounded by a low, white fence hung with colorful flags. At the judge's whistle, a teenage boy in a striped shirt and short pants burst from the starting line, calling and gesturing to a tiny, apricot-colored poodle. Shouts went up from the crowd as the cute canine leapt a series of three fences of graduated heights.

The boy scuttled in front of his pet, pointing and clucking, to put the animal through the prescribed course—up and down a teeter totter, over a water spread, through a tunnel, and then yielding a short pause before a food bowl, without taking a bite. The final, spectacular run contained a bridge, several more fences, and a succession of upright poles, through which the poodle ducked and swayed in the very definition of agility.

Maxi, entranced at the show, gave several sharp barks from the sidelines. The onlookers clapped for the deft display.

"Ohmigod, ohmigod, ohmigod," Sabrina chanted nervously after the flawless performance.

The next contestant, a tall girl of about thirteen, entered with a mechanical German shepherd. Instead of moving through the course ahead of the dog, the youngster stood at one end of the arena and guided the robot with a simple touch behind her ear. The dog's gesture technology monitored every twitch of its handler's finger. Unfortunately, something was either causing interference, or a glitch in the software was creating havoc; the robotic dog interpreted every signal as one to jump. So it tried to leap the teeter totter, tunnel, and food bowl, with varying degrees of success. The pair left the ring to tepid applause. Maxi, eyes on the ring, whined.

The third trial began. Sabrina took a deep breath and announced, "We're fifth. Bam-Bam, let's go," she said, to rouse Mena's sleeping collie.

Bam-Bam did not comply.

"It's time to warm up!" Sabrina nudged the robot with the toe of her shoe, then bent down and shook the thing. The lights on Bam-Bam's collar did not flicker, but shone a dull red.

"What the—oh, *no!*" Sabrina threw Philomena a wild look. Dark clouds built in her eyes and threatened to spill. "He's out of juice. You didn't charge him!" she accused.

Mena just raised her eyebrows. "It's the contestant's job to prep the animal. He's been playing all day. You should've checked him before now, Brin."

Sabrina narrowed her gray eyes, and lightning shot from them. "It's all your fault!" she said, her voice rising hysterically.

"Sabrina Peterson!" George reprimanded.

Jennifer leaned forward to touch Mena's shoulder in mute apology for her daughter's behavior. The third and fourth sets ended, and the announcer called for the next competitors to queue up.

Sabrina took that moment to grab the bracelet that Jennifer had removed from her sticky arm and set on the table. "Maxi: come, girl!"

Before anyone could stop her, Sabrina ran off, with the dog in tow.

"Number five!" came the broadcast.

Sabrina stumbled, and Maxi shot past her, onto the course. The girl jogged after her, then stopped, watching in wonder as the dog took the first three fences, *pop! pop! pop!* Then Sabrina followed, mimicking the jumps and pulling some chuckles from the crowd.

Over the course the little dog went, with her mistress shadowing her moves—scaling the seesaw, leaping the water, and crawling through the tunnel. As the pair lay down in tandem on the pause mat and stared at the bowl of dog food, the audience erupted in charmed laughter. Then the two finished the sequence, with Maxi in front and Sabrina obediently following her through the weave poles.

The applause was so prolonged that they took a victory lap around the enclosure. Once back at the lemonade booth, seeing Jennifer's face, Sabrina wished she could take another lap.

But her mother's wide-eyed expression did not convey the complexity of her emotions at that juncture. And she did not scold her daughter, just held out a hand for the return of the bracelet. In fact, at that moment, Sabrina was furthest from her thoughts.

"Well, I'll be goddamned," Jennifer whispered, eyes trained on Maxi.

Unless she missed her guess, in a matter of minutes, simply by watching, the mechanical dog had learned the entire agility routine well enough to perform it... all on her own.

On her own!

How to hide this accomplishment?

Think fast, Peterson, Jennifer told herself. She scooped Maxi up in her arms. Here came the event judge.

Bryson Burney looked frail and elderly, with his white fringe of hair, stooped shoulders, and his ghostly chicken legs visible between pairs of plaid shorts and black socks and sandals. But his will bore no weaknesses. A dog-show veteran of some forty years, Mr. Burney commanded respect simply by deserving it.

He strode up to Jennifer and Sabrina and motioned them aside from the others. "May I speak to mother and daughter a moment before the results are announced?" he asked.

Flooded with excitement, Sabrina expected praise. Jennifer, flooded with anxiety, did not.

Mr. Burney regarded first Maxi and then Sabrina with disapproval. In a low, quavery voice, he said, "You do know what the penalty for cheating is, do you not?"

Jennifer let out a surreptitious breath. Bonus! To the untrained eye, it appeared that robotic Maxi had simply been programmed to run the course without the requisite cues.

Sabrina couldn't have been more shocked. She opened her mouth to protest, but her mother interrupted. "I don't know what the club penalty is, Mr. Burney. But I do know which family rules apply." She pretended to glare sternly at her daughter, but held her gaze in such a way that Sabrina would know she was faking it.

"I never—!" Sabrina began.

"Young lady," Mr. Burney said gravely. "Do not bother to make excuses. Your performance made clear to the panel that you disqualified yourself by using mechanical means to run the pattern."

"But, I—"

"How can we accommodate both live and robotic dogs if one group has the advantage?" he pushed on.

Jennifer clenched her fists against Maxi, thinking, *Don't argue, don't argue, don't argue….*

Sabrina shut her mouth and pooched out her lips.

To Jennifer's great relief, instead of putting up the usual fight, her daughter burst into sloppy tears. Casting a brief glance at her mother, Sabrina babbled, "I'm—so, so sorry, Mr. Burney. I didn't think anybody would—"

"—would catch you?" he finished harshly. "That doesn't make your misdeed less wrong. Sabrina Peterson, you know better." He drew himself up as straight as he could. "Now. I must return to award the prize… to another." He raised his eyebrows at Jennifer. "I think, in this instance, to preserve today's fun, I'll let you handle the matter on your own. That is, as long as Sabrina finds herself another, more respectable Quest pursuit in future."

Jennifer slid her eyes at her daughter and back at the judge. "Oh, I'll take care of it." She set Maxi down on the ground. "You can count on that."

CHAPTER 11

Sabrina had seen enough live-animal training at the farm in Harmony to recognize organic learning. And she'd known robotic Maxi since she was a toddler, and was aware that—at least, at the dog's programmed intelligence level—robots weren't able to learn. But Maxi had certainly displayed all the signs of having done so, with great success.

So, after the thrill of winning the agility trial and the humiliation of being branded a cheat had cooled, the girl bubbled with questions that only her mother could answer. In fact, Jennifer had forbidden her daughter to discuss the subject with anyone else, for now. But the sooner she faced Sabrina's white-hot scrutiny, the better. It might even help her make sense of all this.

The two Peterson women followed the pedway to OC-3's public zone, a commercial area like the one that lined the canals in Philomena's home city, but with its own flavor. The colorful lights and music of The Alley drew a youthful crowd to virtual shops, cafés, and game arcades. Jennifer did not want to be overheard, and the buzz and bustle would afford more privacy to talk than a quieter space. So she let Sabrina lead her to an upscale coffeehouse with a vertical floorplan that guaranteed an extreme decibel level.

The robotic host escorted them to an open elevator platform that carried them upward, through a space decorated to look like old Seattle. The walls appeared as uneven red-and-brown brick masonry between heavy fir studs, hung with vintage street signs and traffic signals, and an old advertisement for Pike Street Market. Pots of hydroponic trees and stringers of ivy brightened the space, while brass-like railings separated the dining tables. The elevator stopped and hovered near an empty, high-topped table in one of the central lofts.

Suspense had only increased Sabrina's curiosity. No sooner had the robot seated them than she asked, point-blank, "Mom, what the heck happened the other day? Did Maxi come alive?"

The suggestion floored Jennifer—not because she didn't seek that outcome, but because she still could not discern how close to it they had come.

"Nooo," she answered carefully. "I'd say our Maxi achieved a next-level intelligence based on reinforcement. We'll talk about it. But first, we need to discuss your part in all this."

Sabrina sat up straighter on the high barstool. "Mine? You mean besides being a great, big cheater?"

Jennifer could see that, despite earlier arguments about damage to her reputation, Brin was actually enjoying the charade.

They were interrupted by the waiterbot, which also functioned as a drink dispenser. The café's signature drinks were impressively layered in transparent cups for all to see; Jennifer received an iridescent coffee-and-foam tower, and Sabrina chose an orange gelled Italian soda spliced with chocolate cream. They began chipping away at the architecture with long-handled spoons as Jennifer resumed their conversation.

"Brin, you're old enough understand something about Mom and Dad's work that is so important we need to guard it closely."

Sabrina's purple shelf of hair obscured her reaction as she bent over her drink. "I know what you guys do." She raised her head to meet her mother's gaze and returned to her drink excavation.

"But you don't know why we do it. And that's the key to why it must remain secret... at least, for the time being. I'm counting on you to be able to do that." Jennifer regarded her daughter. *Twelve, going on thirty-two,* she thought. If she didn't take Brin into her confidence now, they'd both pay the price.

So Jennifer shared details that otherwise would have waited several years. She told Sabrina about her college studies, recounting her initial interest in creating a "value-added" artificial consciousness—a vast intelligence that superseded human computational capacity but infused its decision making with moral and ethical values. "What good is judgment without compassion?" she asked rhetorically, then realized she'd better make sure Sabrina was comprehending this. "Better yet, Brin, tell me: how does compassion lead to the best possible conclusions?"

Sabrina thought for a moment. Her social studies group had been tossing around some related questions, and to her, the answers all seemed grounded in plain, old common sense. "It keeps people from making selfish decisions," she said. "Like, one person taking all the water during a drought, to drink or water crops. If they gave up an equal amount of water to, say, a dozen people, then all would have some. Maybe enough to stay alive, not just to not be thirsty anymore."

Jennifer let them both mull the concept for a moment. "I'm so glad you said that." She reached over and touched Sabrina's hand. "You just hit on what both your father and I are trying to do with the technology that's unfolding. It's going to give people unlimited potential—but, again, what good is that if only certain individuals can have it?"

"You mean, rich people?"

"Not necessarily. Greedy people. They're always the dividing line between have and have-not," Jennifer murmured. "So, my goal has always been to find a way to embed the best human values in the most advanced artificial thinking."

Sabrina's spoon clinked against her glass. "I'm on board with that." She had experienced enough mean-girl dynamics to appreciate a more considerate way of being. And, thanks to Saturdays at the tech-soup kitchens, she had seen what happened when resources were fairly distributed. "Dad thinks like that, too, right? That's why he's all into public this and public that."

Affirmation seeped through Jennifer's bloodstream and circulated with her pulse. All those years when she thought Sabrina had ignored everything but loud music, she had been absorbing the lessons that Jennifer and George had hoped their children would learn. "Do you know how much I love you?" she blurted out, her heart all but bursting with pride in her daughter's intellect.

"Mom!" Sabrina colored.

"You are so right on, Brin. And that is why I love your father, as well: we both strongly believe that the advancements to come are so crucial to human life that they must be made available to every person on Earth—and beyond, if it comes to that."

"You mean, Mars?" The planet's exploration had been in the news lately.

"Way beyond Mars," Jennifer said, again tiptoeing into a subject that she had not yet risked broaching with her children. "This could be the step that frees humans from earthly or even universal bounds."

Sabrina's forgotten spoon hung in the air in front of her. "You mean, we wouldn't just use technology or let it build itself… we would *become* that technology?" Sabrina's face held a wide and tender wonderment.

Jennifer nodded solemnly. "It's what some people would call evolution."

Now understanding filled Sabrina's eyes. "It's what some people would call God."

>>> <<<

157

Their talk had turned back to Maxi and the agility trials. The robotic pet had witnessed four pairs of competitors round the obstacle course, to various receptions from the audience. Applause and pats were interpreted as positive reinforcement, while a lack of these showed a negative result. What had been amazing, to Jennifer's mind, was that these behaviors were analyzed by Maxi not through her own trial and error, but simply by watching the success and failure of others.

This was a whole other kettle of fish. It implied a cognitive process that internalized action/reaction, and even more amazing, responded to that information with the preferred behavior. In short, it meant that Maxi— AKA Val2001, or any similarly equipped artificial thought machine—could learn to make decisions in a way that heretofore had been the exclusive domain of humans.

"You can see why it would be dangerous for this technology to develop *without* ethical restraints," Jennifer had explained to her daughter. "Or fall into the wrong hands—people who prefer a thought process that excludes morals."

This last possibility hit home with Sabrina as she recalled her cousin Mik's habit of showing off, even if it put people in danger. He'd nearly lost an eye that time, and she or Chris could've been badly hurt.

A cloud passed over her eyes, leaving behind an uncharacteristic fierceness. The child had always cloaked her true emotions. Perhaps, as she grew older, she would be more comfortable in sharing them, however unspoken the concession might be.

Their conversation briefly touched on how Sabrina had handled Mr. Burney's false judgment and how she'd shrugged off the taunts of her club mates who teased her about it. Jennifer had counseled pleading the Fifth Amendment, and Sabrina found that this lent her an air of mystery among her peers. They both agreed that this was the best way to fend off any unwelcome questions—for both of them.

These thoughts flitted through Jennifer's mind that night as she rotated the steel punty on the blowing-bench stand to give the molten glass blob on its tip some shape. The sound system broadcast a romantic ballad loudly enough to be heard over the hot roar of the glory hole furnace. Jennifer swayed a bit to the singer's husky vocals in a language she did not understand, nor care to. Sometimes the translation tool was best left deactivated.

Once more, she bent to her work in the studio, alone, late at night, immersed in her most effective form of meditative thought. As always, that energy was aimed at a problem, or, in this case, a turning point in the solution of one.

Talk about a turning point!

This sentiment applied both to Maxi's progress and Sabrina's—never before had Jennifer entrusted her children with her most precious ideas. These were not their secrets to keep. But, now, circumstances forced her to relax her guard, to have faith not just in Chris's and Sabrina's intelligence, but in their integrity as human beings. Daily life had put her too close to them to notice that they were growing up. Their personal experiences were now defining them, much as the marver rod and flat paddle pressing against the molten glass would yield the finished shape she wanted.

After the family had returned home from the Rendezvous festivities, Jennifer had taken George aside and let him know of her intentions. The time had come to either inform the kids, or inform their bosses at work of what their ultimate goal was, before the truth slipped out. At this point, the couple had more faith in their children's discretion than in that of the still-nascent WLC bureaucracy.

"We might only get one chance," Jennifer reminded her husband. "Once our brand of artificial consciousness is unleashed, we can't influence how it will be used any longer."

George agreed. "From my end, success might be even more tenuous. Certain wealthy interests will do whatever it takes to hoard the ultimate technology. Although there should be no threat. It won't matter how greatly dispersed access might be, everyone will get the same benefits, once we are one."

"But there's no money in universal gain," Jennifer pointed out bitterly.

George bobbed his head. "Only in proprietary gain."

Jennifer had enlisted him to speak to Chris about the matter; their son had noticed Maxi's enhanced performance in the show ring too. Their entire family needed to be sworn to silence indefinitely. Who knew how long they would need to keep the mission's progress to themselves? The conclusive event that would elevate Maxi's consciousness from mechanical to independent—the thing that would make her "come alive"—had yet to occur.

"We'll know when the time is right," Jennifer said, thinking to herself, *and we won't know* what *will happen until it happens.*

She set the half-finished orb in the annealer to cool and pulled out another one to complete, a glass replica of the planet Saturn. All it needed was the ice rings, which she could now attach to the hardened orangish-blue globe. This would be tricky with only two hands; she wished she had an assistant to hold a steady rotation while she wound threads of hot glass around it.

One song ended, and a new one poured into the studio. Bold piano notes mingled with plucked strings and syncopated percussion, in a rich melody that climbed up, down, and back up the scale. Jennifer hummed along with the singer's deep tenor voice. She gave the solid glass ball a deft turn with the tongs as her phone alert broke into the music. She gave the command to answer.

Her mother's voice transmitted. "Jennie, dear. We— we need you! It's your father. He's hurt bad."

A weight seemed to come from nowhere and jostle Jennifer's elbow. The cold glass in one hand and the hot ribbon of silica wielded by the other broke from her grasp. She barely had time to jump out of the way to escape the fallout as the fragile planet of glass—and her world— fell apart.

>>> <<<

The tires and motor hummed over the asphalt. A buckle in the road caused four noticeable bumps—two from bouncing axels on the truck, and two from the trailer it was hauling. Distracted, Jennifer forced her attention on the road and steering wheel. Taking the same route through southwestern Canada toward eastern Montana so many times had lulled her into a self-driving mode. That could get her into a bad accident, and she didn't need another crisis.

Thoughts of her father drifted in anyway. Rip Peterson's morals had immediately come to mind the day before, when she'd had her deep discussion about ethics with Sabrina. Jennifer had to acknowledge her excitement at talking with her daughter about her passion—as equals, maybe for the first time. How often did a parent bring up important subjects with her kids, anyhow?

Sabrina's thought process had practically been visible in her eyes, and rather than challenge her mother's theories, she'd accepted, if not embraced them.

Wow. The kid really was mature beyond her years. In some respects.

Which reminded Jennifer of a similar exchange with her father that had taken place when she was a few years younger than Brin. Maybe she'd been busy honing her scientific mentality; maybe Rip had been testing his spiritual views. Whatever prompted it, the topic of why humans were put on this Earth had come up while she and Rip were out in the mare and foal pasture one day, mending fences.

Young Jennifer sensed that she could ask her father existential questions that her mother might frown on.

"Dad," she began. "Danny Lund said anyone's who's not baptized is going to hell. That doesn't sound fair." She handed Rip a length of wire to use as a splice where the grid fencing had come away from the post.

Rip slid the wire through the lattice and twisted it around the heavy staple in the fence post, from which it had pulled loose. "Well, now. You're baptized, gal. So I wouldn't worry about it." He paused. "Although, you're right. It don't sound fair." He straightened up and motioned for her to follow him down the fence line.

"Well," Jennifer argued, "that tells me that the ones in charge of religion don't know what the heck they're talking about. What kind of god wouldn't be fair?"

They walked a ways, then Rip said, over his shoulder, "Those are two different things. Yes, it's possible—likely, even—that folks laid out the rules wrong. 'To err is human,' and such. As for fairness, we humans can't know what is in God's mind."

The logic escaped Jennifer. "But, just because they might not get dipped in water and prayed on, God would send them to eternal hell? What if it was an accident? What if they were sick that day and then, quick, died? What about if they weren't in a baptizing religion? Why would God say all the *other* nonbaptized Jewish and Hindu and other people couldn't get into heaven, on a technicality?"

She heard Rip chuckle. "Well, I don't claim to know what hell is like. Or heaven, for that matter. I think what is important—baptism or no—is that God forgives folks of their sins."

"But how can a baby sin?"

Rip stopped and knelt to look over another suspect patch of fence. He cast his daughter a quick glance. "We can't know everything, Jennie. Only what's true of people. And to err *is* human."

"Then why can't people just forgive people? Why can't that be enough?"

"Because we aren't the whole equation, right? There's something more out there. And, as Bill Shakespeare said, 'to forgive is divine.'"

This sounded definitive enough that Jennifer had abandoned the line of questioning. But she couldn't help but think that her father was giving God more than the benefit of the doubt. People of distinct faiths did think their beliefs were the only true ones—that everyone else was wrong. Did her father think this? It didn't seem like it.

But, while he was a man of faith, he was also a humble man. He admitted what he did not know. Most grown-ups would never do that.

Jennifer thought—now, some twenty-five years later—that Rip would have made a good scientist. Her mother, on the other hand, was convinced that everything she needed to know was written out in the Bible. There weren't any gray areas. She'd be the type of researcher who drew conclusions first and then searched for evidence to back them up.

Jennifer herself had softened, over the years. As a teen-ager, she'd decided that an absence of certainty equaled the nonexistence of a higher power. But this type of assumption, she had learned in her studies, did not jibe with the scientific method. Learning to accept ambiguity—with optimism, not cynicism—had brought her to where she was today.

She smiled, thinking briefly of her friend Philomena, who would've hated that creed. "Agnosticism," she had once told Jennifer, "is for skeptics who are too chickenshit to be atheists." Maybe she was correct. But, as a scientist, Jennifer needed evidence. She'd have to remember to tell Mena that agnostics have a right to withhold judgment, but the burden of proof was on the atheists.

Anyway, none of that would matter someday, when the ultimate intelligence gained consciousness and pulled humankind together. Jennifer approached a line of vehicles and slowed the truck and trailer, thinking that whatever rifts separated folks couldn't be healed fast enough for her liking. She'd almost reached the border.

CHAPTER 12

The car in front of Jennifer's truck backed up slightly, wheeled into a U-turn, and screeched off, back up Route 2, into Alberta.

Denied entry.

Jennifer's knuckles went white on the steering wheel as she edged toward the Ameristates inspection booth. A light rain fell, and the brown-uniformed woman inside seemed inclined to stay under cover. Perhaps she was worried about her makeup running; thick concealer under her eyes only accentuated their bags, from which an even thicker coating of neon-cherry lipstick could not distract attention. The inspector tucked a string of brunette hair back under her brown cap and wordlessly reached for Jennifer's passport. No facial scan here, as the more efficient and advanced Canadian border system used to positively link travelers to the biometric chips in their official papers. If anything, Ameristates' technology had backtracked; digital approval had been replaced by the old physical rubber-stamp practice.

In a monotone, the guard demanded an additional photo I.D. Jennifer handed over her cell phone, with the correct frame exposed. She wanted to make this crossing as conflict-free as possible.

The guard returned the device. "Record of business transaction?"

Jennifer flipped to another frame that displayed a notice of equine sale and held it out for her to see.

The woman hesitated, then set her unholy lips and stepped from the booth to look over the trailer hitched to the big hybrid truck. She stepped up to the driver's-side window and barked, "Where's the horse?"

Jennifer clutched her phone more tightly and displayed the sale page again. Why did they always seem to ask the wrong questions?

"I'm on my way to pick it up. I'm the purchaser," she explained, hoping she wouldn't have to show proof of ownership of the vehicles. She'd borrowed them from her friend Laura, who lived on the outskirts of the Olympic Cities.

The ruse had worked before. Ameristates had closed its borders to tourists two years earlier, delaying the Peterson and Xical families' annual get-together. The isolationist tactic soon backfired. Having broken so many of its trade agreements, the Grubb administration needed some way to shore up the economy. So business deals became a provision of international travel—just one more way to milk foreigners and keep Americans dependent on the state. Jennifer, George, and the kids had feigned horse buys twice already, making up for lost time.

But one never knew what would happen at the entry check. So, when Ruby called with news of Rip's accident,

Jennifer had left the family at home and set out eastward, alone.

A sale that hadn't been completed yet was tough for the border police to disprove. The force of company men and women wasn't really trained to evaluate business travelers' claims, anyhow. But if Jennifer were detained and the matter looked into, Rip's legitimate status as a horse breeder would've lent credence to the deal. A couple of long, suspicious looks and one cash transaction later, the guard shoved open the wide, wheeled gate, and the Jennifer guided her vehicles through.

She drove south on the Montana state highway until she was out of sight, and then pulled over onto the shoulder. She was trembling, and forced herself to take several deep breaths.

Receiving her mother's call two nights before had caused a similar physical reaction. In the meantime, spending more than twenty-four hours to make what had once been a twelve-hour trip was nearly unbearable. She phoned home to Harmony during the layover in Calgary and got Grant on the line for an update. Their father was still at the hospital in Billings, and, as far as he knew, still unconscious from a fall. Jennifer planned to drive directly to the city, but early the next morning, Grant had called her to say that Rip was awake and had been released.

"But, shouldn't he be, like, monitored or something?" she asked.

"Skull fracture, concussion, more than sixteen hours knocked out... you'd think they would," Grant answered. "They say the brain-bleed has stopped, and they set his wrists and casted 'em, but he's run through his allotment of pain meds, and he doesn't have a health savings account, so they're booting him. Or maybe it's not the doctors booting him, but Grubb giving him a great, big kick in the ass." He took a breath. "The government is rot."

It hadn't improved any, Jennifer had to agree. But the president and his cronies weren't the ones to suffer. They had commandeered fuel supplies and skewed taxes to keep their planes and cars and private hospitals running. Meanwhile, Grubb's stubborn reliance on fossil fuel and strongman trade tactics had steadily chipped away at ordinary folks' reserves and supply chains. Jennifer encountered more evidence of this as she cruised through Harmony's main street: The water tower had never been resurrected, and more shops were shuttered than open for business. The only conveyances on the street were pedal powered or horse drawn. Even the flashing light at the four-way stop had gone dark.

If the scene was this depressing to her, how must the residents feel? Jennifer flashed on her father's frame of mind. The man had always soldiered on, never complaining, just adapting—swapping wheat farming for ranching, letting his horses pull the hay mower and baler once the gasoline ran out. What would hold him together now? She stepped down on the gas pedal as hard as she dared, to erase the distance that remained between them.

>>> <<<

"That boy has been such a blessing," Ruby Peterson said, nodding at Sheila's teenage son, Mik. They sat stiffly with Jennifer in the farmhouse living room, all of them worn out from the episode. "What with Grant taking on more of your father's chores, and your father less...able—" she choked, the greater truth of her words overcoming her composure. She broke down in quiet sobs.

Before Jennifer could rise and go to her, Mik sprang across the living room and knelt at his grandmother's side, squeezing her arm. "Sshhh. No worries, Grandma. You can count on me."

Jennifer added, "Dad's already on the mend, Mom. You know what a tough cookie he is. He'll be back at it in no time." She looked at her nephew, pleased that he'd stepped up and chipped in when they needed him. Now seventeen, he might easily have other priorities.

Ruby dabbed at her eyes with a tissue Mik provided. "I know he will, if the Lord sees fit. I'm just worried for the day they call Grant into service. He's already used all the deferments he could get."

Jennifer cocked her head. "Isn't he a little old for that? He's forty-three, for Christ's sake."

Ruby clucked, warning her daughter not to blaspheme, but Jennifer hardly noticed. "What's the rule now?" she asked, adding to her nephew, "I take it you're not old enough yet."

"Gotta be eighteen. Which I will be, in about a month." Mik moved across the room to a side table that Ruby had set with cookies and iced tea. He helped himself to a couple of cookies. "But there's no upper age limit. They could call Grandma and Grandpa next."

"Oh, come on." Jennifer was shocked, but not surprised. President Grubb had fewer and fewer resources to plumb these days. In fact, their family had already been tapped for national service twice, with both Sheila and her husband, Ron, having pulled Western border patrol duty for weeks at a time. The on-again, off-again marriage was back on, as the two needed each other's means to stay afloat: Ron's income from a hauling business kept the kids' mouths full, and Sheila's home in the farm compound kept a roof over their heads.

"I can't wait till my turn," Mik said through cookie crumbs. "Dad says being a company man is a blast. You get to go through boot camp and everything."

Jennifer eyed him sideways. "Like boot camp is fun."

"Well, you get to travel, and meet up with a bunch of guys and girls. Watch for crooks. Shoot guns."

It sounded a lot like a domestic army, to Jennifer.

"Dad says if you show your loyalty, you get special perks—like a gas allowance, Internet access, travel privileges. That kind of thing."

Just then, Sheila, Ron, and the girls, Liz and Dora, came through the front door, without knocking. Sheila was sipping a jumbo-sized soda. The kids were arguing about a toy.

"Hey, keep it down," Jennifer admonished. "Grandpa's sleeping."

"Well, look who's here!" Sheila said, implying *it's about time.*

Jennifer got up to hug her sister, and as an afterthought, leaned over and let Ron kiss her cheek. "Nice to see you two." His breath smelled of unbrushed teeth, and the stubble of a two-day beard scratched her skin. Tall and wiry, Ron projected the seen-it-all nature of an ex-con, which came across in the set of his face and tight posture. An armful of blue tattoos sticking out of his black T-shirt could have been self-inflicted, or just meant to appear so. If he had done prison time, it hadn't kept the government from calling him up. What did Sheila see in him? The bad-boy persona didn't wear well on a man his age. His thinning, brown hair stuck out from under a red COMPANY MAN baseball cap, a souvenir of his days in public service.

Ron looked around the room and fixed on Mik. "You've been lazing around here long enough. Get home, boy."

Mik scowled, but didn't move.

Then, as if he cared, Ron asked Jennifer, "Where's hubbie and your 2.4 kids?"

Mik caught his eye and said pointedly, "She left 'em at home, along with the dog."

Besides shielding George and the children from an interrogation, Jennifer had left Maxi behind, safely stashed in the wall safe in George's office. She'd heard rumors of arbitrary searches and seizures at the border. Crossing into Ameristates with the valuable files would have been too iffy. She had also become worried about Maxi's stronger signal being picked up by anyone interested enough to notice it, and the strongbox at home would help deflect any wireless probes.

"I decided not to risk bringing the whole family across the border," Jennifer explained. "If one of them was denied, I'd have to turn back too. And I wanted to be here for Dad."

Sheila said curtly, "Sure you did."

A call from the next room acknowledged Jennifer's presence. "Did I just hear one of my favorite daughters mention my name?"

Jennifer smiled. "He's awake."

"You keep the kids in here," Ruby told Sheila and motioned for Jennifer to follow her into the bedroom. Ron trailed after them.

"Dad!"

Rip Peterson lay in the queen-sized bed, which had been pushed against a corner of the room in the absence of guardrails. Several lumpy pillows had been placed around him in an effort to keep him still. He wore tan pajamas with light stripes that matched his blue eyes, and a thin blanket was pulled up to his chest. Jennifer reached down and gave him an awkward hug and kiss.

"Didn't expect you here," Rip murmured.

"Didn't expect you there," she joked gently. "Grant said something about a ladder, and that you hit your head and broke both wrists. What the heck happened?" The terse telephone conversations and brief chat just now hadn't done enough to fill her in.

Rip turned his head, then winced. "What's that?" He was having trouble hearing.

Ruby spoke up. "Your father's getting too old to climb ladders. He claims to have missed a step when it folded up on itself."

Rip seemed to search his memory. "Could've sworn I locked the durn thing."

Jennifer's stomach roiled as she tried to picture the scenario. "But, where were you? What were you doing?"

Ron supplied, "He was trading out light bulbs in the stable. Our boy, Mik, was right there." The man only seemed to claim his stepson when it bolstered his own image.

"That was a blessing," Ruby repeated. "Him and Grant got Dad into the wagon and off to County. Lucky for us, they had an ambulance on call that day. Don't have the right machines for a "cat" scan in Harmony. They took him all the way to Billings, and he never woke up." Her voice quavered.

"Till morning," Rip put in, awareness of the timeline showing that his faculties were returning. "Best nap I ever took. Then they kept waking me up on purpose." He gave a weak grin.

This cheered Jennifer, but she was still disturbed that it had taken so long to get him the care he needed—and that she couldn't be there to hold his hand, or her mother's. "I wish you'd moved West with us a long time ago," she confided to her father. "It'd be a lot harder now, if you'd even be allowed to emigrate."

"Oh, I couldn't leave the farm…."

Ron coughed. "Ameristates are in a big human resources push. Got to capitalize on our biggest assets—working people."

"Somebody's capitalizing, alright." Jennifer shook her head. "What this country needs is renewed infrastructure—starting with an investment in new technology."

"Now you're talking, sis-in-law," Ron agreed. "Could use some of what you-all have out West. Maybe we wouldn't have to work so hard and could take it easy, like you."

Rip intervened. "We do okay. Who needs fancy gadgets when you've got horsepower?" Again, a weak chuckle.

For a moment, no one backed up his optimism. Then Jennifer touched his pajama sleeve. "That's right, Dad."

He was ever determined to be happy with what he had. But she could see it wasn't enough.

>>> <<<

Jennifer stayed until her father regained his hearing and got up and about. With both wrists in casts, he still needed help in and out of bed and chairs, but at least he was able to walk for a few minutes without getting dizzy. His daughter, however, was developing symptoms of her own. The forced hiatus from her work had worn on her patience. So, to get out of her head, she spent as much time with Grant and the horses as possible.

It was shoeing day again. This time, Jennifer held a male horse steady in the barn doorway for Grant, who bent over the gelding's right forefoot, trimming away with a hoof knife. He had removed the old shoe, and once he had evened out the overgrown hoof wall, he would reshape the shoe and nail it back on.

This was the type of precise, step-by-step work on which Grant thrived, and it was crucial to the health of the Petersons' herd. The black, heavy-bodied horse named Nod stood about 15.2 hands—an ideal size for pulling the harvest implements and the manure spreader that fertilized the hay field. Attention to hay growth and harvest year round kept the farm self-sufficient, as a portion of the nutrient-rich grass could be swapped for the grain that the working animals also needed in their diets. Regular hoof care every six weeks kept the horses sound and performing well.

The work was accompanied by the distant *pop! pop!* of gunfire. Outside, Ron and Mik practiced target shooting back along the tree line. Nod, used to this soundtrack, paid it no mind. Grant set Nod's trimmed foot down and grunted, straightening up.

"Looking good," Jennifer encouraged him. "You sure are one busy guy, bro."

Right now, with Rip laid up, Grant was doing it all—caring for the horses and hay field, as well as monitoring the in-foal mares and training the youngsters for sale.

"Sheila's boy helps some, with the stalls and feeding. I think he's just trying to get out of the house, though. There's been some squalls between him and Ron, ever since he moved back in."

"There's still so much work. Don't you worry about getting called up for national service?"

"Nah. Just wouldn't do it. This is what I do." Wasting no time, Grant started trimming a hind foot.

Jennifer wondered what the consequences for ignoring the service draft would be. In another time, Grant's condition would excuse him from public duty. But the Grubb years had not been kind to those with disabilities of any sort. Jennifer imagined the citizenry were used like young racehorses—run hard and thrown away when they no longer won races.

"So, you're no company man, huh?" Jennifer joshed, trying to keep the mood light.

"All a ruse. All a ruse." Grant's voice was muffled as he doubled over the hind hoof, trying to dig out some foul-smelling thrush. He motioned for Jennifer to hand him a bottle of medication, which he applied to the grooves around the soft underpart of Nod's foot. "This 'service'," Grant continued, "is advertised as serving the national interest—protect borders, protect farmland, protect things that don't need protecting. So they've got folks with guns running all over the place, authority to shoot illegal travelers, shoot wolves, shoot whatever else moves if they don't like how it's moving. You think anybody wants to get into this country any more—legally or illegally? Not a chance. And, you shoot the wolves, you get too many deer. You shoot whatever else moves, you get people afraid to leave the house. *That's* what the real aim is. All a ruse. All a ruse."

"But what's the point of that? So folks are scared of Grubb and his pals. What does that gain them?"

"That's the ruse. That's the ruse. It looks like the national service corps are helping folks, while they're just a smokescreen for the real company men—the ones doing the kind of dirty work that doesn't need guns. Spies. Infiltrators. Deal makers. These are the real company men." Grant set the hoof down and turned to face his sister. "I look like one of those to you?"

Something in his expression tore at Jennifer's heart—it held a mix of disgust and defeat she'd never seen in him before. Again she wished she had convinced him and Dad and Mom to move West when they'd had the chance. Sheila would've gone along, too, if somebody had arranged everything for her. She tended to take the path of least resistance and had never entirely stood on her own feet. But, she might have just as easily have stayed on the farm, if they'd left it to her.

Suddenly, Grant's attitude changed, and a light entered his eyes. "Hey! Remember that horse-shoeing machine you were working on? Whatever happened to that? I could sure use it now."

"The horse-shoeing... ? What're you talking about?"

"The god machine. The one that can do everything. Even farriery, right?" He picked up the last, untrimmed hoof.

"Oh. That." *Jesus, that was two-three years ago.* Jennifer barely recalled their conversation at the river that day. How much had she told him? "I'm... closer to getting all the data in place. That's one thing. Getting it to fly on its own is the next step. The final step."

"Well," Grant said, speaking to the stable floor again, "I know you can do it, Jens. I'm thinking that machine of yours could be what our country needs right now. You said it'd be nice—that means, it'd know right from wrong. That's what we're missing. That's what we're missing. We're missing it. I remember when it wasn't so."

The note of despair had crept back into his voice, touching Jennifer. "I remember, too." She felt such a decisive jolt in the pit of her stomach that she yanked on the lead rope, startling Nod, who tugged his hoof away from Grant's hands.

Grant swore, just as Sheila's husband, Ron, stepped into the barn, unannounced.

Again the horse spooked at the sudden movement, this time pulling back against the rope that Jennifer held. The animal skittered in place, and then raised a hoof and stamped down hard. It landed on Grant's foot.

"Owww!"

Jennifer glared at Ron. "Call out when you're around the horses!"

Now Nod, stiff-legged, didn't want to move, and he had Grant's boot pinned to the ground. Grant writhed helplessly. Jennifer shoved herself into the horse's hindquarters to throw him off balance. He shifted, and Grant pulled his foot free and staggered against the wooden barn siding.

"Gotcha!" Ron said, unapologetic.

Grant took a look at his COMPANY MAN hat and grimaced. "Take that thing off!"

Ron ignored him and instead addressed Jennifer. "Heard you're leaving soon. Can I get a ride to town?"

Grant stomped over and grabbed Ron's hat by its bill. "It's my stable. I said no hat!"

Ron got ahold of Grant's wrist and wrestled with him. "No hat! No hat!"

"Guys!" Jennifer gave up some lead rope as poor Nod backed away from the ruckus. She released the horse and dove for the cap that had fallen to the floor. She thrust it at Ron. "You need to go. Now!"

Her brother-in-law narrowed his eyes and lunged at her, then thought better of it and pulled away. "You'll be sorry."

It was a strange threat to make over a hat. Was it meant for her, or for Grant? Her brother—odd, smart, sweet, vulnerable Grant—was still an easy target. Now Jennifer played the familiar role of defender, as she'd done so many times during childhood. "How could you? Get out!" She flew at the retreating Ron and made sure he was out the door before turning back to assuage her brother.

Nod bolted past them, lead rope flying. Grant knew better than to run after a fleeing horse, but Jennifer could see he wasn't worried about that. Her brother stood rooted in place, jutting out his chin and snaking his neck in a series of ducks.

Uh-oh.

She saw an unhealthy glint in his blue eyes, as though something had popped—like the lid off a trash can. Emotion started to spew out. "Don't go. Jens. Jens. Jens. Jens!" Grant picked up the tools at his feet and threw them all at the wall, making a racket.

"I'm not going," Jennifer murmured.

"He said you are!" *Wham!* Grant knocked his head sideways against the wooden boards.

Jennifer stayed silent, balling and releasing her fists. *Wham! Wham! Wham!*

She saw a small trickle of blood break out on his temple. It was all she could do not to run and get him in a headlock. He'd only overpower her. As with Nod, it would do no good to try to stave off whatever held Grant in its grip, until he came to his senses.

After a few more whacks, he stopped banging against the wall and collapsed to his knees. Eructations of sobs seemed to rumble through him from deep underground, shooting outward like geysers. His tears quickly washed away the blood on his face, and his body vibrated with shivers that tried to purge him of some unseen toxin.

Still, Jennifer did not comfort him. She waited out the anguished cries, which diminished and then abruptly cut to nothing as Grant scuttled around on the ground to face the wall. His shoulders shook, his voice had dwindled to whimpers that were subdued, but anything but quiet. Jennifer imagined that, inside, the rage was still alight. So she waited.

Neither of them knew how many minutes passed with Grant's wires crossed, whatever mental or physical needs within him striving for fulfillment. No matter how many times Jennifer observed his meltdowns, each one was horrifying—at base, a loss of control that no man or woman ever wanted to watch, let alone experience. But someone needed to make sure Grant didn't hurt himself too badly, and the only thing he wanted at such times, he'd once told her, was her presence. No judgment, no solace—just understanding.

At last, he began to stir. He unfolded his rigid legs, pushed against the wall, and rose, still not looking at Jennifer. He hung there for a while, conversing with another world. Then he started muttering to himself, a mixture of angry and tired proclamations aimed at no one.

This was the hardest part for Jennifer. She knew she had to let him come out of the episode at his own pace—to reach into her own reserves to stay calm and pretend nothing special had happened. All the while, she couldn't help but feel that she'd sorely failed her brother. She could drop in and out of town, in and out of his life, in and out of her own obligations, on a whim. He was the one with no say in things.

When, at last, his monologue tapered off and he cracked a sideways glance her way, Jennifer, muscles rigid as well, dared to move. She saw a bright ribbon of euphoria cross Grant's face, the sure sign that he'd gained whatever it was he'd been looking for.

"I'm hungry," he croaked.

She reached out and tapped his sweat-soaked back, then massaged it briefly. "Go on back to the house and get something to eat," she said, with deliberate nonchalance, barely under control herself. "I'm gonna go catch that horse."

PART III

NEW YORK (AP) – NEW YORK CITY DECLARES INDE-
PENDENCE FROM AMERISTATES

WASHINGTON (AP) – AMERISTATES ENDS FUNDING
FOR BIOENGINEERING RESEARCH

MOUNTAIN VIEW (AP) – WLC CONSIDERS
FAST-TRACKING BIOPARTS APPROVAL

CHAPTER 13

April 16, 2032

George Xical braced his hands against his shiny, black desk and listened to the stream of rhetoric from the WLC spokeswoman with one ear. He'd already heard all this once before, at the most recent annual congress in Sequoia. His presentation on additive manufacturing had been pooh-poohed by some of the higher-ups, and the same argument was replaying now. This tactic of repeating things in an effort to make them more true, or more palatable, was one of the elements of working for the government that he liked the least, and which he hadn't expected.

He had probably been naive to think that the emerging WLC democracy would evolve in a vacuum, free from the red tape and spin cycle of Washington. But, back in 2020, idealism had been running hot. After secession, those in the Western states thought improving on the U.S. mess would be slam-dunk. The shared losses in the Mexican war had thrown a sheen of unity on a population that was, perhaps, more diverse in its thinking than anyone realized.

And, so, George steeled himself and said nothing while the press liaison finished her spiel.

"So, you can see, Secretary Xical, that we still don't have the support to mandate fund matching for A.M. At this juncture, public access will remain optional."

The image on his desk screen showed an energetic older woman dressed, like George, in a blue and green WLC rugby-style jersey. The connation that they were part of the same team began and ended there, today: her last words told George that the two years he'd just spent on additive-manufacturing access had been a bust. This didn't bode well for the next project.

George pulled his collar away from his throat, which did not relieve the constriction. "Then, Ms. Ramirez, you realize we will go straight to the tax committee in the next session. The hell with matching funds. We'll ask for a straight-up tax cut on biological parts, and we'll get it." He hit the desk, trying to mask his actual lack of certainty. The progress in 3-D printing of human tissue had made his department's efforts even more critical to the WLC's stated mission of resource equity.

Ramirez drew herself up and said haughtily, "You're going to get it, alright. Powerful people want to keep this technology out of the public sector. Sec-Gen Pierce ran on a neutral platform over the issue, so she's not about to fight for it."

George's earpiece signaled an incoming call on his private phone. "I must cut this short, Cristina." He signed off and tapped his earpiece, then strode out of the office, to leave the bad news behind him.

In the hallway, he nearly tripped over Maxi, who circled in place to avoid him. When Jennifer's stay in Montana had stretched past a week, George had given in to Sabrina's outrage and let the dog out of his wall safe, with strict instructions that she remain in the pod. It did seem more like home with Maxi patrolling the place. He didn't bring up the topic, or the tussle with the secretary-general, with his wife now. The conversation was short, and he'd finished it by the time he arrived in the kitchen to find Chris and Sabrina dining on lunch burritos.

"Mmm, smells good," he said. "Hali-shark?"

Chris nodded.

"I just spoke to your mother. She's been delayed."

Sabrina set down the fish and black bean–filled zeppelin. "Is Grandpa alright?"

"Sounds like he will be."

"How much longer is Mom going to take?" Chris, now sixteen years of age, wanted to know. Jennifer's absence relieved him of maternal scrutiny but added responsibility for Sabrina's whereabouts, and the fourteen-year-old did not appreciate the arrangement.

George fiddled with the dinnerbot. "I don't know; she's stuck in Canada. The truck needs a fuel pump. Maybe three days."

"Three days!" Sabrina flipped a slice of long, green hair over her shoulder. She'd let it grow out for some time, and had trimmed it at an angle—halfway down her back on one side, up to shoulder length on the other. "What, is Mom riding old Madeline all the way home?"

George entertained the prospect as he brought his plate to the table. "She could do it, as the crow flies." He frowned. "She'd need an armed guard to get through Indian territory, though."

"Cowboys and Indians. That sounds so retro," Sabrina commented.

"No joke," Chris said. "The Nations have gotten militant about protecting their space." Chris got the scoop from his Makah friends, who all monitored the goings-on in the Ameristates reservations.

"Well, nobody else is going to uphold their sovereignty," George said. "Grubb certainly fell in line with the old U.S. practice of screwing over the Indians."

"Why don't they just form their own countries, then, like the WLC or New York or Hawaii?" Sabrina wondered.

Chris knew the answer. "Location, location, location. Most Eastern reservations are surrounded by non-Indian lands. Think of which states joined the Western Core—the ones on the edge: Cali, Oregon, Washington, Arizona, Nevada. Then New York City opted out—on the opposite edge."

"They say half of New England will be next," George added. "But, consider Hawaii—islands with a strong indigenous heritage. Their location was definitely the deciding factor. They were able to secede given their buffer zone in the Pacific. It would've cost Grubb more than it was worth to fight over them."

"The Lakota and other Native Americans don't have that safety net," Chris pointed out. "Even if Grubb did cut 'em loose, it's not like they can live off the land anymore… at least, not well enough to sustain their numbers. Even if they could survive a war."

This drove them each into their own thoughts for a few moments.

George worked away on his burrito at the glass table as Chris and Sabrina pushed back their plates and drifted off. Maxi gave a sharp bark followed by a plaintive, *Oooh-ooo, oooh-ooo!*

Forgetting the dog's post-dinner protocol, George assumed she was missing Jennifer. He gazed at her through the glass. "Don't worry, girl. Mom'll be back soon."

>>> <<<

It took more than three days. To Jennifer, that equaled a lifetime on top of a lifetime. Even with all of the stuff going on in Harmony, the urge to move Maxi up the intelligence ladder beat like a drum in her head. And after the time off, James Ting would have his own plans for her. Ethics had been flooded recently with requests for waivers to let certain bioengineering processes bypass the system. *The faster things advance*, she thought, *the quicker they expect approval.* It had been a dozen years since the WLC had adopted its ethics codes. Back then, support had been strong. Researchers knew they were on the cusp of game-changing technologies. Now, nobody seemed to want to wait around for reports on pesky details like their impacts on humanity.

This was the very situation the Core administration was supposed to defuse. Scientists had predicted exponential growth for decades, and the opportunity to prepare for it was to be the saving grace. Besides the goal of tempering effects was the mission to equalize access—to put moneyed interests second to these priorities. Now it seemed like both of those objectives might fall by the wayside. Twelve years of progress could be quickly erased—unless a bridge was built to link the two goals. Maxi could be that bridge. Jennifer was sure of it.

Ironically, that project would have to wait. Right now, she had a bigger problem to deal with. The front-door sensor identified her, and the transparent panels parted to let her pass.

"Mom's home!" came Brin's voice from somewhere inside, followed by more than one pair of footsteps.

The entryway suddenly crowded with Petersons and Xicals. As the luggage rolled in after Jennifer, Maxi hurtled forward, yipping with joy, her claws tapping on the tile with excitement.

In that instant, all other movement ceased. Jennifer stared at the dog. Sabrina, Chris, and George stared at Jennifer—and beyond her, to where a young man hung back in the hallway.

"*Day-um*," Sabrina exclaimed.

Maxi sniffed the guest and growled, unsure about him.

George looked the boy up and down, murmuring, "Guess who's coming to dinner, right?"

It was Mik.

>>> <<<

Nobody was sure who exploded first, but Jennifer's reaction was loudest. "What the goddamned hell is Maxi doing out?" She trained her ire on her husband.

It was catching. George waved at Mik. "What in *el nombre de Dios* is *he* doing here?"

"Is it legal for him to travel?" Sabrina asked.

"Of course it's not, stupid!" Chris snapped.

The four family members faced off, sniping at each other while Maxi twirled in circles and the automated bags blindly followed Jennifer to and fro. Meanwhile, Mikhail, Sheila's son by her first husband, took in the scene, trying to decide whether to enter the fray or not. He finally sauntered into the pod and threw back his head, turning in a circle. Then he walked over to the sleek, black couch and seated himself, only mildly surprised by the footrest that elevated out of the floor in front of him.

"Nice place," he said, sticking out his feet and letting them drop onto the footrest.

Chris heard him through the din. He touched his mother's arm. "How'd you guys get over the border? Come on, Mom. What's going on? Give us a clue."

Jennifer was still livid about her files roaming freely about the house. Before she could switch gears, Mik spoke up. "Hey, cuz. You're looking at a bona fide political refugee, seeking asylum."

"Looks like you've got a roommate," Sabrina shot at her brother, who opened his mouth to argue. "Well, he's not staying with me," she declared.

"Why don't we trade? You've got the bigger room."

Sabrina crossed her arms. "No way."

This line of reasoning was not lost on George, who suddenly realized that a young-adult male, vaguely related or not, should not be bunking with his teenage daughter. "There's always the couch...."

Mik, already comfortable there, said, "Fine with me."

Jennifer's usually pale face had gone a hot shade of pink. She bent down and scooped Maxi up in her arms. "Not fine. Mainly because: we're moving, folks. As soon as possible."

If they hadn't been surprised before, her husband and children were definitely floored by this statement.

"Wait a second—" Chris was still trying to make sense of his cousin's presence. "He's gonna *live* with us?"

George knifed a glance at Jennifer, silently repeating the question.

Through tight lips, she replied, "He is. And we're moving out."

It was Sabrina's turn to go frantic. "We're moving... just so Mik can have his own room?" Her voice rose precipitously. "But all my friends are here!"

Mik raised a hand and said sarcastically. "Don't worry, Brin-Brin. You've got me now."

Explanations flowed in fits and starts, like curdled milk from an old, cardboard carton. The reason for Jennifer's nephew's sudden appearance in their living room could not wait, so she laid out the short version: the boy had secreted himself in the tack room of the empty horse trailer that Jennifer was hauling back home. He'd remained there, underneath a pile of saddle blankets, until after they'd passed through the Canadian checkpoint. The officials there had seen no reason to search the rig, once Jennifer's papers checked out and she told them that her purchase had fallen through.

When she pulled into the motel at Calgary and got out of the truck, she'd heard an intense thumping coming from the little corner tack room. Alarmed, she'd peeked inside and found Mik. In just a thin shirt and jeans, even under the cloth pads, he was thoroughly chilled from the ride through spring hailstorms.

Before she could ask, he defended himself. "R-Ron said he was gonna kill me. I had to get away. I believe he'd do it, Aunt Jen!"

Of course, Jennifer had been shocked and angry at having carried a stowaway across international boundaries. More perplexing was his stateless status; he had no legal standing to travel through Canada *or* to enter the Western Land Core. But she realized that the boy must have been desperate to pull such a stunt. So they'd hunkered down in Calgary while Jennifer pursued their options.

"What about the option to send him back?" George demanded now, as though the boy weren't sitting right there on the sofa.

"Feds wouldn't have liked that," Mik put in. "Americans who flee the country are called turds. As you could guess, turds aren't welcomed back with open arms."

"But why are you a… turd?" Sabrina pressed. "Besides the obvious," she added.

Jennifer had calmed down a bit, and her expression softened. "Now, Brin. Your cousin was threatened by his stepfather. He literally feared for his life, and he took a chance. When I discovered him, he asked for my help." She looked at George, imploring him to understand. "He asked for shelter. I couldn't say no."

Mik thrust out his chin with dignity. "Thank you, Aunt Jen."

Jennifer said ruefully, "It may have been part my fault. I had a fight with Ron that day that may have set him off. He's the type to lash out. He might've taken it out on someone else."

George listened soberly to all this. On the one hand, he was deeply disturbed. His wife had lied to him about the truck breaking down. She'd performed illicit acts that could have gotten her sent to jail, and then concealed what was going on when he talked to her on the phone. On the other hand, she hadn't had much choice. What was she supposed to do? Abandon the boy? Start a long-distance row? He had to admit that she'd done what he would have done—helped the boy get clearance for asylum in the WLC, and taken him into their home. At least, for now.

Jennifer told them that she'd ignored calls from Harmony, letting her folks think her cellphone had died. George mentioned that he'd passed along the story about the truck when they got ahold of him.

After some more discussion, he caught his wife's eye and said quietly, "You did the right thing. But I think you owe us some input on the idea of moving."

"We talked about that, hon," Jennifer reminded him.

"You *did?*" Sabrina was flabbergasted that she hadn't been consulted.

"Yes, well, that was awhile back," George admitted. "And we certainly weren't thinking about adoption."

Mik eyed his uncle and aunt. "I'll be eighteen a few weeks," he said defiantly.

Jennifer took a breath. "That's neither here nor there, for the time being. The reason for moving has to do with security." She addressed her family: "Now. Will someone please own up to letting Maxi out of the safe?"

At this, Mik looked confused, but intrigued. "You keep your dog under lock and key?"

It was George's turn to confess. "I gave in to the wrath of Brin, Jen. She accused me of being cruel and heartless by keeping the dog in a dark box for so long."

"Maxi's a robot!" Jennifer burst out, her agitation growing again.

"Grab ice, Mom," Sabrina pacified her. "I remembered what you said. Besides… I kept her batteries charged up."

>>> <<<

Sabrina couldn't have known that hooking Maxi up to the wireless system was the last thing Jennifer wanted. *I should have been more specific,* she thought, now worrying as much about her daughter, son, and husband as her four-legged data receptacle. Any number of corporate and foreign spies would be looking to capture the breakthrough technology she was cultivating. The danger to Jennifer and her family had grown very real.

At the same time, when Sheila and Ron learned of Mik's whereabouts, they might retaliate. After talking these worries over with George—and arguing about the tradeoffs—Jennifer got his consent to go ahead with moving plans. They would give up the family pod in OC-3 for a slightly larger floor plan in one of the "primitive" smartcities, the ones marketed to people who, for one reason or another, wanted to live off the grid. This meant no dinner robot, no remote office, and no Internet.

When she heard the news, Sabrina clutched at her throat. "Buy me a human recycling permit, then. Without the Internet, I might as well be dead."

Even Chris couldn't fathom independence from his online networks. He tried to play on parental concerns. "How'll we do our homework?"

Jennifer dismissed their anxiety. "You won't miss out. OC-12 has a separate islet for wireless activity. Every kid on the place will be there." She appealed to Sabrina. "You'll probably make more friends than ever. I hear they've got a professional recording studio."

"Yeah?"

"Look at this as a chance to do more of the things you already like. Chris, that SCA group meets there," she informed him.

"What's that?" Mik asked, idly searching for a way to exploit his cousin's contacts.

"Society for Creative Anachronism," Chris explained. "They re-create feudal society and battles and stuff."

Jennifer saw the lights come on in Chris's eyes. Her son's interest in historical weaponry had been stoked during his time with the Quest League, and he'd been wanting to join the local medieval society, to get into jousting and broadsword combat. Even Mik appeared mildly interested.

"But, what about Maxi?" Sabrina asked. "Are robotic pets even allowed on OC-12?"

Jennifer had checked into this. "As long as they're life-like," she answered. "That means no 'soft paws' features or designer species hybrids. We're lucky Maxi's a real Aussie dog replica." Not that Jennifer would have given her up anyway. The kids weren't even aware of what she and George would have to sacrifice for the move—he'd go back to commuting to OC-1, and Jennifer would lose proximity to her glassblowing studio. On top of all that, someone would have to shop for groceries and cook. She put some much-needed spin on this detail. "Won't it be great to have a real kitchen? We can all take a historical cooking class."

Mik, who hadn't entered the debate yet, saw a chance to make points. "That's where I come in," he said. "You haven't lived until you've tasted my barbecued brisket."

Sabrina looked skeptical. "What's that?" The family had subsisted on the dinner robot's pizza and burritos for as long as she could remember.

Mik smiled at her smugly, glad to have the upper hand for the first time since leaving the farm. "Grandpa Rip's recipe. You'll see." He bent down and stroked Maxi's side, then fingered her collar, turning it around on her neck as though to see how it functioned.

Jennifer thought to distract him from the dog. "Come on, Mik. I'll show you around."

CHAPTER 14

Chris rode the underground bus from school to the new OC-12 pod, watching the virtual above-ground scenery projected on the bus windows as it went by. He liked commuting. This must be what it felt like to have a real job, not just volunteering at the soup kitchen or play-acting mountain man with his Quest buds. It made him wonder what he'd end up doing. He'd be graduating in a couple years. He'd only thought about what he'd *like* to do with his life, not what was possible. Were they the same things?

Basically, he'd always wanted to go back in time. In centuries past, people had been forced to rely on their wits, and their hands, and old-fashioned skills that had visible results. A man could live off the land, even in isolation. That kind of self-reliance seemed eminently satisfying.

These days—and surely for the foreseeable future—cooperation and dependence were unavoidable. Not that those were bad things, but each compromise that adults had to make seemed to suck a little bit of gratification away. Even consequences were shared. Chris had never noticed this dynamic until he moved up in the Quest hierarchy. He'd been groomed from childhood to find the middle ground in any conflict and to accept any difference of opinion. But in the Mountaineers branch of the club, he experienced what it was like to build skills that made him less reliant on others, not more. If he failed, he paid the price. Sure, they'd all done their citizenship and volunteer duties—civic cleanups, hospital visits, and the like. But it had been the hard stuff, the individual badge pursuits in graduating from Trapper to Trader to Explorer that captured his imagination. He didn't care that the means to these ends were virtual; what he'd learned was real—like knowing the habits of animals in order to set proper traps, and how to make a living trading the pelts for necessities that he couldn't get in the wild, like flour and salt. Having tasted these fundamentals, it was hard to get jazzed up about the things his mom and dad wanted him to do.

He supposed that Jennifer and George expected him to get a nice, clean, boring job with the WLC or some charity group. They'd devoted their efforts to the common good and had clearly raised him and Brin to adopt that work ethic. Oh, nobody called it work anymore. What used to be called *employment* was now referred to as *investment*, which was all about the future. Frankly, Chris thought the future was overrated.

What the heck's wrong with now? he silently asked the bus window. If life on "primitive" OC-12 was sustainable, why couldn't he just live it? Their new neighbors seemed into it—having barn dances and potlucks and quilting bees, or whatever. But then they all went off to day jobs, or social pursuits, working on big plans for tomorrow. Maybe his contribution could be making *now* valuable again.

He twisted in his seat. Of all people, Mom should understand. She'd come from a place where generations had worked the land, letting sunrise and sunset dictate their days. It was what he loved about visiting the farm, and why he'd been excited to have his cousin Mik move in with them. Mik was a real guy—he burned things and shot things and knew what it was like to get beat up. Chris had pictured the two of them as a team in Mountaineer contests or as foes in medieval melees at the OC-12 Renaissance fair. Instead, his cousin had ditched him for a new group of friends. And Chris couldn't stand them.

Sure enough, when he entered OC-12's Buzz Zone, the city island's offshoot that floated in Lake Washington, there they were. Two young men of about Mik's age flanked his cousin, who sat at a wireless station he had claimed as his own. His friends looked ordinary enough— white guys with ruddy complexions, cut-short hair, and burgeoning physiques under their summer shirts and shorts. But they acted different from the older kids Chris knew. Their uninhibited speech and habit of staring down anybody and everybody suggested that they didn't give a damn about personal boundaries. The world should clearly bow to them, and not the other way around. While Chris found tolerance a pain sometimes, he still considered it a necessary societal evil.

"Get a load of Mr. Lady," the shorter one said, pointing at an image on the desk interface. Chris drew closer, and he saw it was Secretary-General Pierce. The most recently elected WLC leader was a woman with a no-nonsense bearing that some people criticized as unfeminine.

The taller guy snickered. "Bet her shorts are full. Put that in Comments, Mik."

"Bulging is more like it. But let's talk about her face." Mik had become something of a celebrity with the group, and now appeared to be in charge.

Shame by association enveloped Chris as he watched his cousin append animal names to the distinguished woman's online resume. He was about to walk away to another station when Mik noticed him. "Hey, Chrissie. You like monkeys, I'll bet. What're those ones with the face that looks like a dong?"

Chris paused. "Don't you have anything better to do?"

"No. I don't. President lover," Mik said derisively. "Or—what's the fake term, Fabs?"

The short guy pointed to the photo caption. "Secretary-General. Just one of dozens of secretaries running this country. Taking notes. Pouring coffee."

"Hey." Chris couldn't let that slide. They were crossing into family territory. "My dad's a secretary."

Mik offered false support. "And George Xical is a big name in welfare promotion," he informed his buddies. "It's what this great land of yours was founded on."

"*Ours*," Chris corrected him. "You're supposed to be getting your inclusion card, remember?"

"Right. There's going to be a civics quiz," the tall guy needled Mik.

"Shut up, Miller. We'll see who's laughing when I sell my I.D. to the highest bidder back home."

Sheesh, Chris thought. The guy hadn't been here a month, and he was already on his way to a life of crime. "What do you owe anybody back in the States?" he couldn't help asking. "Where were they when you needed help?"

Mik reached out and put a hand squarely on Chris's face and pushed it, rudely. "I got here on my own steam, dingus. Maybe it's them who need my help."

"Company men forever," the guy called Fabs said, and the other two echoed him. They lost interest in Chris and turned back to the social page they were denigrating.

So much for Mom rescuing Mik from Ron and national service, Chris thought. What would George say if he knew how ungrateful his nephew really was? Look how much trouble they'd all gone to, to make him feel safe and welcome. In a way, though, this alleviated Chris's own disappointment. He didn't want to hang out with Mik now, anyhow.

Chris went over to the family locker, intent on pulling his cellphone from the charger to make a few calls. Then he spied a girl he liked from the fair committee. She was practicing her double-handed sword maneuvers up in the glass-enclosed holographic loft. She was pretty darn good. Maybe it was time to ask her out.

>>> <<<

Sabrina hadn't told anyone, but she thought her cousin Mik was cute. Had she just not noticed before? Or had he recently grown into what she considered the ideal body? From the ground up, he was what movie/rock stars should be: legs that showed hard calf and thigh muscles; ab and chest peaks like deep moguls; a broad back sliced by a sexy ravine; and arms that looked like they could lift the sky. His lips stuck out just enough. His eyes were hidden by a permanent squint. Sabrina and her friends at the rock gym agreed they could climb up and down his cheekbones all day long.

Of course, she would never tell him that.

Instead, she wanted him to feel it—to feel her attraction to him in an equal and inexorable pull. She set out to make this happen.

They'd moved into their new pod, or cabin, as the rustic OC-12 homes were known. Mik seemed so at ease in a place with solid-wood doors that you had to push open and pull closed, and a kitchen with foreign, dangerous-looking appliances. When the hardwired telephone rang, he knew how to answer it. When nobody could find the garbage chute, he got up and took the bag outside.

Mik was sitting in the living room listening to his favorite country singer one day when Sabrina came in and stretched out on the floor nearby. She had put on a stretchy blue shirt with see-through sleeves that looked great against her current peach-and-magenta hair. She took the long end of her hair and wrapped it around a wrist until Mik sensed her presence and peeked up from the paper magazine he was flipping through.

"What's with the clown wig?"

This wasn't the response she'd expected.

He cocked his head. "Come to think of it, cuz, I don't even know what color your hair is. Every time I see you, you've got some new Crayola job."

"Well," Sabrina said with a coy note, "what color's your favorite?"

"I like blondes."

What a break!

"I *am* blonde," she told him.

He gave her a yeah-right look and went back to his magazine.

She reached over and flicked a finger at it. "Where'd you get the antique?"

His dark-brown shock of hair fell over his brow as he hunched deeper into the couch, ignoring her.

After a moment, she read off the cover, "*Personal Home Defense.*" The graphic showed two glowing red eyes staring out of a thicket of brush. "What's that—some yard and garden thing?"

Exasperated, he flashed the centerfold at her. It was a glossy photo of an L-shaped pistol with a silver trigger and a black-matte finish. "Government Model 1911 Defender, five-inch barrel, tritium sight," he recited, and raised his eyebrows at her.

"Arctic," Sabrina said admiringly. "Could you teach me how to use one of those?"

He snorted. "You've prob'ly never even used a letter opener." Her silence told him he was right. "Look. You start out with knives."

Yes!

Sabrina mentioned that Chris had won a real throwing knife in a Quest competition. He sent her to hunt it up. Then they went outside.

Mik carved a diamond in the bark of an alder tree. He backed up a ways on the grass and spent some twenty minutes flipping the knife at the target, not saying much, just swearing when he missed.

Watching closely, Sabrina learned how the weight and trajectory affected the knife's aim. When Mik didn't offer her a turn, she grew impatient. "How about letting me have a try?" She put out her hand.

He dangled the knife, then swished it away when she grabbed for it. "I've got a better idea." The cabin faced a neighborhood park that spread out on the other side of the wide, gravel public walkway. A few kids played on the swings there next to a wooden gazebo. From its eaves fluttered a string of triangular plastic flags. Mik jutted his chin at them. "Those'd look good in my room," he said. "See if you can't climb up there and cut 'em down."

Sabrina eyed the structure. It was encircled by a lattice fence to form walls that went about halfway up to the roof. She could climb on that and reach up underneath, easy. "Okay."

She took the knife, ran over, and swung onto the balustrade. Grasping a support beam, she rose to her feet. Then she let go and balanced, stretching for the flag cord with one hand and slicing at it with the knife. Her heart jumped when it snapped loose. "I've got it!"

She dropped down and sank to her knees, then turned to show Mik. Her heart plummeted when she saw he'd already gone back inside the cabin.

She felt liquid pool in her eye, and vexed, swiped it away. She was *not* going to cry. As she gathered up the flags, the little kids swarmed over to get a look. One of them pointed at her and said, "Whoa! You're bleeding!"

Sabrina looked at her damp hand, which showed red blood, not tears. "Yeah, yeah. I must've cut myself." But there was more blood. And then more.

Sabrina started to freak. "Is it coming from my *eye?*"

The kids' stricken faces told her the source didn't matter as much as the volume. Sabrina ran for the house.

>>> <<<

Jennifer had to admit, the move had not been drama free. George grumbled about his new office on OC-1 and let her know what a martyr he was being, for her sake. Chris had a falling out with Mik, and Sabrina had come home one day with an awful gash just over one eye that took forever to stop bleeding, but hadn't needed laser sutures.

With peace somewhat restored and the family settling into a new pod, Jennifer returned eagerly to work. Jack16 had plenty of pending human-resolution cases for her to review. At the end of a long day of deliberations, with most of the department gone home to dinner, she finally turned her attention to Maxi's hard drive.

Her goal had been to hit a Z-RAM ceiling sometime within the next three years, based on the department's average data flow. With maximum data saturation plus a synthetic neural implant, a wholly distinct artificial consciousness might no longer be a dream. It had been ages since she'd run a diagnostic check. She shut down Maxi's main program to initiate a scan. "Let's see where you're at, girl."

After a day of close work, Jennifer was content to hang out in the lab and wait for the tool to run through its sea of code. She sat back, idly watching the lights on Maxi's collar pulsate red and blue, her curiosity and impatience rising. Every now and then, she got up and paced the room, then sat back down again. With the unauthorized data pulls over the past couple of years, her projected saturation timeline had shrunk—but by how much, she didn't know. When would the years of waiting end?

Perhaps, even sooner than she thought. The lights on Maxi's collar went dark, and Jennifer brought up the results of the completed analysis on her desk display. She scrolled to information she was looking for, and froze. A tingling sensation spread through her body. Without another thought, she initiated a file transfer from the closest storage device, which happened to be Jack16. Then she ran the diagnostic again.

There was no sitting still now. She prowled the room like a caged lion, every cell of her body seeming to vibrate. She watched the collar lights for so long, their blinking afterimage remained in her vision for several seconds even after they'd faded and gone dark again. Then she dashed to the desk display.

Thanks to Sabrina, while Jennifer had been away, Maxi had devoured information off the Internet, stashing it neatly in her hard drive. As the small robot's database had grown over time, Jennifer had incrementally added memory cells. But even Z-RAM transistor space was limited. And, the diagnostic report indicated, it had now reached that limit. Again, she read off the finding in terabytes: *Used space, 200 TB; Free space, 0.*

Holy shit! Now what?

This was as far ahead as Jennifer had thought, assuming she still had a few years to get her final preparations together. She'd need a contact at Mountain View's bioengineering campus, a way to reveal her achievement to key players in the Pierce administration... and a way to conceal it all up until the right moment. *Wait till George hears this!* Or, should she keep it under wraps, even from him and the secretary-general, until she was guaranteed the necessary security and adherence to the WLC mission?

It was impossible to know which would be the right track to take.

Then a thought occurred to her. The Ethics lockdown! It was filled with genetic replicas of human body parts that were awaiting evaluation and ethical clearance. Physical specimens were required, not just the backup data.

She checked the time; it was late, but that was a good thing. She could end this all tonight—right now.

Still, she hesitated. The tingle of excitement went cold, as a chill wind of reality swept over her. The implications of an autonomous artificial consciousness were vast, the technology priceless. People would kill for it—would threaten those she loved to get to it. Even in the solitude of the high-security laboratory, Jennifer had never felt so exposed.

She glanced over at Maxi lying on the floor, then reached down and stroked her soft, synthetic fur. Would she remain a pet? Or become a tool that could profoundly elevate the human race?

A scene entered Jennifer's mind, of the faithful acolytes performing their spiritual rituals on the lawn at the park, the day she'd played tennis. As George had suggested, in their own ways, maybe they had all been searching for the same thing. What if the focus on their differences was what held them back? She may have been right about their shortcomings—that they were based in competition and ignorance. But those weren't irreversible motives. She knew; she had the data right here in this room to back that up. What if the technology gestating inside Maxi *was* capable of overcoming those negatives and freeing people who were trapped in their thinking by fear or ignorance?

George had asked a similar question that day. His words of encouragement came back to her: *You change 'em, Jen.*

She patted Maxi's soft fur once more, then rose on unsteady legs. It was up to her.

Without warning, the lab door clicked and slid open. Her boss, James Ting, stepped inside.

"Jennifer. I thought I'd see what you were doing here so late...." His voice trailed off as he glanced over her shoulder at the desk interface. He leaned closer to view the diagnostic figures.

To Jennifer's knowledge, no one in the department had ever compiled that much data in one machine. She knew her boss knew that, and would wonder why. She saw his posture tense with suspicion. Then something else caught her attention.

Down on the floor, the dead lights on Maxi's collar illuminated. Her eyes cracked open, glinting dull silver. Jennifer gasped.

Ting gripped her shoulder. "You're through here. I think you need to come with me."

CHAPTER 15

Maxi shuffled around the board room, red and blue lights winking from her collar. At a time like this, Jennifer usually could rely on the dog's company for some kind of consolation. Now she eyed the robot warily. *What the hell is going on?*

Good things… don't worry.

Jennifer started. Had she just said that out loud?

Her throat felt so tight that she doubted if she could speak right now. James Ting had escorted her to the meeting room, instructing her to wait, and closed the door. It might as well have been a prison cell. Certainly, if Jennifer tried to leave, she'd either have a guard after her or an immediate dismissal. So, what was her next move? What was Ting's?

Jennifer's inner scientist took hold. *Okay. Let's review. Who knows what?*

At the present moment, nobody but Jennifer knew she'd hit a data ceiling of her own choosing. And what did it consist of? Good question. The bulk of the information related to how ethical decisions were made—but

Maxi had sucked a wide variety of intel off the Internet, at times, over the past few years. Topics could range from social posts about whose kids were doing what, to how to build bombs—and anything in between. This stuff wasn't necessarily detrimental; it all reflected the diverse input that humans got, which helped to form world views, motivations, and future plans. On the downside, though, it was rife with prejudices and misinformation, things that reasonably intelligent people could identify and take with a grain of salt. Could a machine distinguish this type of fiction from fact? *Maybe.* If not, when it became capable of independent action, it might act from a poorly constructed ideology. But, if so... *it would so fuckin' rock!*

Jennifer didn't want to get ahead of herself. What would all this matter to her boss, and his bosses? Number one, Ting didn't know for sure about any of this stuff, even if he suspected Jennifer might be working on something on the side. Number two, the department's security had already been breached by an unidentified leaker. Admin would probably connect Jennifer to that crisis. So, she was looking at one immediate danger: that they'd name her as the mole. If she could find out who was behind the hacking, she'd be in the clear there. But that would take time.

And a little poking around the lab right now would tell Ting that the 200TB data mass did not come from any of their machines. That would make Jennifer appear to be a thief. Was there some way around that?

To explain the abnormal, she had to look at what *was* normal.

The Department of Ethics ran cases for government-regulated activities with potential human impacts apart from economic ones—like those with consequences related to the environment, those that favored or disfavored different social groups, or those with risks of fatalities. The software included thirty-two major ethical markers that formed the basis for a decision matrix: *if this, then that.* Issues that could be resolved within this framework were handled by Jack16 and his crew. Any that fell outside that scope were bumped up to the supervisor—Jennifer. Could she fabricate some rationale for gathering only those human-input resolutions? Something that would explain why she'd need a megafile of that size?

Her articulated thoughts melted to pure internal inquiry.

Meanwhile, Maxi curled up at her feet.

It was well into the evening by the time James Ting brisked into the room, without bothering to knock. "I've just spoken with Sequoia," he said, meaning the capital higher-ups in the Pierce administration to whom he reported. "They've asked me to revoke your security clearance. I told them I'd get your statement first… and go from there." He sat at the head of the table, shoulders sagging slightly, and wearily rubbed his temples. The room's bright working light bounced off the silver streaks in his black hair. He regarded his lab supervisor for a long moment. Then he drew himself up to his usual full-upright position and said—much more gently than expected, "Jennifer. We've worked together for a long time. I've never known you to display even a pinprick in your solid integrity. I'm afraid I am seeing that now." He paused. "Am I wrong?"

Although she hadn't compromised the department's intelligence, Jennifer knew that her priorities no longer jibed with Ting's. Hazy guilt clouded her reasoning. Should she come clean with him? Or further mask her objectives?

What would George do?

Again Jennifer gasped. She hadn't been thinking about her husband… but his work did offer a plausible distraction. Or, at least, a direction in which to divert Ting's inquiries.

"I appreciate your giving me the benefit of the doubt, James," she said, hoping that saying so would make it so. "I'll admit to you, I have gone… offsides. But I haven't gone rogue on you."

He whooshed out a breath. He wanted to believe her. He waited for an explanation.

"Can we—take a walk?"

Ting's expression asked why.

Jennifer tugged at an ear and raised her eyes to the ceiling to suggest their conversation might be overheard.

He nodded.

>>> <<<

Jennifer may not have given her boss the whole story, but it was time to let her husband in on it… most of it, anyway. Especially now that she'd involved him. Jennifer woke George; he'd already turned in by the time she and

Maxi came home. As she got ready for bed, she gave him her account of the day's events at the laboratory, including the excuse she'd used to mollify James Ting.

"*Jesucristo*, Jen!" He sat up against the pillows. "Sure, the bioengineering lobby has been vicious, but do you really think they've been surveilling Ethics?"

"Well, somebody has. And we're up to our ears in bio-medical waiver requests. So it seemed like a good 'out' to tell Ting I've been safeguarding our reports on those cases."

"What the hell did he say to that?"

"He... wasn't pleased. But, then again, he said he couldn't fault me. He'd put me on notice months ago that someone wanted sensitive information from the department; he just didn't say what kind, or why." Jennifer moved over to the chair where her pajamas lay and started to undress. "Why wouldn't I have been cautious?"

George rolled over to face her. "Do you think Ting bought it? That you're not a spy—that you're trying to shield the department against one?"

"Well, it depends. He asked me to hand over the redacted files. I said no."

"What th—? *Por Dios*, you're kidding."

Jennifer slipped into silk sleep pants and a matching top, then ran her fingers through her hair. She turned and approached the bed again. "I said I'd sent the files to a secure cloud location, and that I'd return them once we'd plugged the leak and found the source." She hesitated, wondering how much to share. "But, George. Let's put that on the shelf for now. Do you know what just happened?" She plopped down beside him and grasped his forearms, gazing into his dark eyes. "We're *this close!*"

She took a deep breath and let him go, wriggling into bed. She patted the mattress, and Maxi hopped up and maneuvered to the space at their feet, where she always rested. Then Jennifer looked at her husband again, reliving in her mind the shared journey that had begun so long ago.

George basked in the expression in his wife's eloquent, violet-blue eyes. They seemed to contain all of her passion and persistence on this mission, an undertaking that would've stymied any other human being—in fact, it had done so, up until now. No one else, to the couple's knowledge, had even approached this level of ethics-influenced artificial intelligence. No one else would've had the guts to stick with it, George thought, or the selflessness to devote a lifetime to it. If anyone could lend a moral consciousness to a superior thinking machine, it was Jennifer Peterson.

He didn't realize that she might have already succeeded.

>>> <<<

For all his brash pronouncements, Mik Peterson was highly observant. In the past, it had kept him one step ahead of a thrashing. Now, keeping his ears open seemed not just prudent, but potentially lucrative.

The move from Aunt Jen's OC-3 pod to their present rustic confines had given him a great advantage in his search for marketable information: a lack of soundproofing. He'd been annoyed by this feature, at first, when Sabrina's god-awful music leaked out of her room at all hours. But tonight, it was giving him exactly what he wanted.

Muted voices came from Jennifer and George's bedroom, next door to the office that Mik had entered for listening purposes. He sidled up to the heavy, synthetic-log wall that the two rooms shared. The wood was so realistically rendered that the corner joints sported large cracks—the kind that, in an actual cabin, would alleviate stress but not weaken the construction. For Mik, they doubled as intercoms. He took care to stay quiet as he eavesdropped. The voices rose and fell, subject to movement in the other room.

"… someone wanted sensitive information from the department… just… what… or why," he heard his aunt say.

"Do you think Ting bought it? That you're not a spy…?"

This was interesting. He strained to hear, but her words were unintelligible. He couldn't tell what George's reply meant. Then Jennifer's voice rose again.

"I said I'd sent them to a secure cloud location, and I'd return them once we'd plugged the leak and found the source."

This nearly stood Mik's hair on edge. Leaks? Sources? Was this the hacking mission Ron had been talking about? Mik was so involved in speculation that he missed her next phrase. But he caught the tenor of excitement in those that followed: "George… do you know what just happened? We're *this close!*"

Mik heard somebody stir and footfalls heading toward the door. Picking up his feet deliberately but swiftly, he slipped back into the hall and made it to his bedroom, two doors down, as he heard the knob turn. Someone padded into the bathroom.

The teenager was no fan of Ron Jones, but his stepfather's "in" with the company men promised to make life better for the both of them. Ron's zeal helped keep Mik informed—the man couldn't help but divulge what was supposed to be inside information. Mik sighed. Whether he stayed here in the West or drifted back to Montana or elsewhere wouldn't matter much. A guy like himself could do Ameristates a lot of good. He'd give his stepfather a call in the morning.

Mik wasn't sure what his aunt was up to, but the puzzle pieces were starting to arrange themselves of their own accord. All he had to do was wait, watch, and listen.

>>> <<<

Jennifer did not sleep much that night. Her job hung in jeopardy, which put access to the department storehouse of bioengineered tissue on shaky ground. Even if she got into it, would she know what to look for? There probably wasn't a big, red sticker that said SYNTHETIC BRAIN CIRCUITRY on it. Of course, she wasn't even sure exactly which "parts" were needed, or how critical life-support functions would be. Assuming Maxi's intelligence level was equal to or beyond human capacity, she—or he, or it—would be able to continue amassing the information needed to develop further. At that point, Jennifer would no longer be of use; intelligence past that peak would be out of her league. She had done all she could to instill the malleable human emotions and morals necessary to think and use thoughts positively. She could only hope those efforts would be enough.

The gray zone—the other functions of the human brain that would allow Maxi to break free of her control and act on her own—was still sufficiently foggy. Jennifer felt she'd hit a wall, but that it wasn't insurmountable.

Let me help.

She jerked in the bed, then willed herself to relax, so she wouldn't wake George. This was the third or fourth time she'd heard the timbre of her own voice in her head! Either she was becoming more sensitive to her inner dialogue, or...

She let that thought dangle in her mind.

The alternative, which she'd only let scrape the corners of her consciousness, was that Maxi—or more precisely, the cognitive entity within Maxi—was beginning to... Jennifer didn't want to say communicate, but at least *emanate* its thoughts. It could be using the bioengineered earpiece that Jennifer had been wearing for as long as she could remember as a bridge, a conduit. Another electric surge tightened her muscles. *Jesus, Peterson! Are you seriously believing this?* But, then, how could she not? She had "seriously" been anticipating a developmental stride like this. She just didn't know how it would manifest.

She felt around at the bottom of the bed with a foot until it met Maxi's dormant form. A familiar rush of affection for her pet filled her chest, augmented by something more. What was it?

Jennifer gave up trying to keep still. She reached for her bracelet on the bedside table and pressed the Follow Me button, and then, quickly, the Mute command. Then she slid out of bed and out of the room, with Maxi behind her, leaving George to dreams.

Woman and robotic dog passed soundlessly across the hall rug and through the kitchen, which was far enough from the sleeping chambers that Maxi's claws against the hardwood floor disturbed no one. Jennifer found a coat and slippers near the back door, dressed, and led the dog outside.

Night splashed its indigo ink against the late-summer sky and spattered the canvas with silvery stars. Between the neighborhood cabins, against the horizon, tall fir trees stood out in darker relief. As Jennifer's eyes adjusted, she made out the lines of the ornate gazebo in the park across the way. "Come on, girl," she said, and led Maxi over the gravel and short, crisp grass.

Out here, in the open, the constellations were recognizable overhead. Jennifer automatically took inventory, noting the stair-steps of Cassiopeia seated above Polaris, the north star. Below that spread part of the Big Dipper, obscured by the gazebo's rooftop. The star formations made her think of Grant, and their father. Both men had always watched the stars, part of the wisdom shared by the *Old Farmer's Almanac* to clue them into good planting sequences. Jennifer had finally checked in by phone with Ruby, to make sure that both Rip and Grant were doing okay. She'd held off on news of Mik, since his immigration status hadn't yet been finalized—and since Sheila assumed he'd run off to join up for service the moment he turned eighteen. Jennifer silently begged the distant celestial bodies to watch over them, and the rest of her family.

She led Maxi into the gazebo and knelt next to her, stroking her soft back. Again, the sensation of familiarity came to Jennifer, along with another layer of emotion whose meaning she could not grasp. If only she could ask the questions that she'd carried with her for so long, or—better yet—ask for answers to them, because she'd certainly expressed them plenty of times in the past twenty years, to no avail.

Jennifer's sentiments swelled and arched over her like a silk parachute as she ran her hand over Maxi's slick fur. It no longer seemed strange to direct such devotion to a replica of a living being. "Do you know how much I love you?" she murmured.

And then, so clearly there could be no mistaking the sound, she heard an answer, in her own voice.

Yes.

CHAPTER 16

Another forced vacation, this time dubbed 'paid administrative leave,' had left Jennifer at loose ends, with little but her whirling thoughts and emotions to occupy her time. George's days away from home were longer now. Chris and Sabrina had after-school activities, and Mik had found a new circle of friends who rarely left the Buzz Zone. Meanwhile, Jennifer fretted. James Ting had pushed her out of the laboratory while her story was vetted. *Don't hold your breath on that one, boss,* Jennifer mused as she made her way to the gondola station on OC-5.

Instead of elevating Jennifer's concern over Maxi's safety, recent events had reassured her that, on some level, her pet could take care of itself. So, she had few qualms about taking Maxi along on a hastily arranged date with Philomena Fine. She still synced the dog's collar to her bracelet, but the measure seemed more habit than requisite.

There stood Mena, in a long, floral dress and wide-brimmed straw hat, alone. She must have left Bam-Bam at home. Jennifer waved and picked up her pace.

Despite the sense that Maxi was safe in public, Jennifer did not want her conversation with Philomena overheard. A nice, long gondola ride promised an ideal solution. After hugs and pats, the trio waited their turn in line, Maxi panting and jittering in place, as her program dictated in excitable situations. Like any real dog, Maxi adored the type of forward locomotion that a boat or car afforded. Her scent application would keep her busy deciphering odors from one of the, Jennifer mentioned to Mena, she'd be sticking her head out to catch a breeze.

A self-piloting gondola pulled up to the dock and let them embark. Maxi bounded aboard and propped her front paws on the side of the boat—one of the long, thin, shallow crafts that dominated OC-5's canals. Philomena punched in a scenic cruise on the keypad, leaving their destination open.

The passenger station where the two friends met lay across from Mena's favorite café in the commercial district. They set off downstream, away from Lake Washington and toward Puget Sound, passing sleek holographic fashion-display houses and toney office complexes, all decorated in some innovation of Italianate style. A riot of flowers spilled from the hydroponic boxes along the route.

The channel scene afforded sharp contrast to life in Jennifer's new home city. While the vibe here was Old Venice, the underpinnings were purely state-of-the-modern-art. Moving water held an electrostatic charge that acted as an air cleaner for the immediate environment. That slight smell of humid decay was false, Jennifer knew, spurted from hidden vents like atomized perfume. The waterway also served as a clean-energy source for local transportation and for exercise, evidenced by the cargo barges, canoes, and kayaks that went with the flow. The canal, however, was no one-way street; it divided below the water line into two courses, one that poured upstream and one that ran down.

They rode in silence for a spell. When Jennifer seemed loath to break the mood, Philomena took a crack at it. "Sistahfriend. You're hiding something from me. You know I hate surprises." She elbowed Jennifer, who sat beside her, looking like a tourist in a Olympic Cities T-shirt, shorts, and sunglasses. "Come on, spit it out."

Where to begin? Philomena was hip to Jennifer's and George's converging missions regarding advanced intelligence technology. Her previous skepticism had stemmed from the idea that such accomplishments lay eons in the future. Perhaps it was time to quash that myth.

"Mena, I've got something to tell you that'll rock your world. But it's going to send tremors everywhere, and there are people who won't like it. I need you under oath today."

This earned a classic evaluatory look from Judge Fine, who decided that Jennifer was not kidding around. She raised her right hand and said, "Lay it on me."

Jennifer reached out to steady and subdue Maxi, whose wags threatened to topple her out of the boat. "I think we've reached a tipping point, Mena. We, meaning Maxi and me, George and me, the Western Land Core ethics department and me." Her voice dropped to a whisper. "Girlfriend. I think I've done it."

The jurist did not appreciate ambiguity. "Done *what?*"

Slowly, Jennifer put the situation into words. "I believe I've… finally managed to… approach the next step in human evolution."

Philomena's head snapped back, and she tossed a wild glance over each shoulder, to see if anyone else had heard. Her hat tilted over one eye, causing a bit of tucked-up silver hair to come loose from underneath. "Holy motherfuckin' shit, woman." She took hold of Jennifer's dark glasses and raised them up, so she could drill straight into Jennifer's eyes. "Are you saying what I think you're saying?"

She let the glasses fall, and Jennifer nodded.

"I have every reason to think we're on the verge of moving AI to AC."

Impatiently, Mena said, "Lose the acronyms. Do what?"

"We're a hair's breadth away from giving artificial intelligence a separate, artificial consciousness." Jennifer shuddered at the finality of this statement.

"Damn it, Peterson! Layman's terms: do you mean you're about to bring a fucking machine to life?"

Mutely, Jennifer nodded at the wiggling Maxi.

Philomena's mouth dropped open. "You mean, *her?*"

A grin winnowed its way across Jennifer's face, and she allowed herself to enjoy the ebullience that she'd been suppressing. "Yes! And no. It's… complicated."

Her obvious joy was contagious. Philomena gave a deep chuckle. "Always is, with you science types. Give me the simpleton's version."

With an immense feeling of release, Jennifer launched into a more technical explanation than was needed. The gist of her near success was clear: she'd made a major step, maybe the penultimate one, toward her driving aspiration. Jennifer defined that as enabling the accrual of enough information for an artificial being to compute, solve problems, and learn from experience on a human scale—in a way that was shaded, but not curtailed, by emotion and moral awareness.

Jennifer burned with excitement. "It's possible that this entity already has an intellect beyond our bounds, or soon will."

Philomena, a bit unsettled by the prospect, regarded Maxi. "You mean, she can learn? Outside of her programming?"

Jennifer affirmed this, and Philomena clucked her tongue. "I should've known. I saw her run that agility course, the day Bam-Bam crapped out. We all just assumed it was an act dreamed up by Sabrina." The wind rose across the canal, and Mena jammed her hat down on her head. She tilted her chin at Maxi. "So, she can learn. And understand good and evil, basically."

Jennifer nodded again.

Philomena peeked at her sideways. "How do you know?"

Oh, dear. Jennifer had been afraid of this. Of course, her judge friend would want proof. The woman did not trade on faith.

"I... she..." Jennifer tried again. "I heard her talk."

Mena drew back. "You mean, you told her to speak, right? And she... barked. Or maybe something a little more off-program?"

Jennifer shouldered into her, conspiratorially. "Mena, I heard her *say* something." She sat up and met her friend's dubious gaze. "In—in my head."

"In your head," Philomena repeated.

Jennifer had nothing to add. They sat quietly for a bit as their gondola floated through the transition district. Here, wharf businesses, commercial fishermen, and seagoing boats clustered along the canal inlet that linked the lake to the sound. A few seagulls cried out overhead. A brown pelican beat its wings and settled onto a dock pylon.

"Okay," Mena finally said. "You're Jen Peterson. You're not a nut… you're not a Jesus freak. You wouldn't presume to interpret the unknown unless you had a damn good reason." She paused. "So, where does that leave us?"

Jennifer felt a rush of affection for her stalwart friend and gave her a quick hug. "It leaves us on the edge of the precipice, Mena. And I need your advice."

She summarized the perils of the moment—the threats from government and corporate interests who would want to appropriate Maxi's technology, and the difficulty that her job suspension would cause in seeking out the bioparts to finalize her quest. "I'm scared, Mena. I admit that. But there's no way I'm giving up now. I just don't want to blow it, and breaking into that lockbox is my best hope. It's also highly illegal."

Philomena thought this over. "I get that you can't exactly ask for police protection. But finishing the job and going public would do the trick. Is there anyone in Ethics or Citizen Welfare who can help?"

"That's the problem. I'm really not authorized. And now my sec clearance has been yanked. I'd be criminally liable…."

"… if you get caught."

"If I get caught."

A gleam entered Mena's eye. "And you want me to rule on this ethics case?"

Jennifer realized she'd been trying to pass the buck for her decision. "What would you do?"

Another gray-and-white seagull hovered over the canal, loosing its invective. The wharf quarter had given way to a chain of residential pod complexes. Philomena turned halfway around and punched an about-face command into the gondola's navigation system, to head them back downtown.

She turned back to Jennifer. "Fuck Ethics," she said. "Get what you need. I'd go take that shit."

>>> <<<

Mik knew when Chris and Sabrina would be returning from their Quest League meeting and went to meet their bus on the lower level of OC-12.

"Oh, hey," he said casually, pretending he'd exited another car. "You guys going to Buzz Zone?" He also knew that they always checked their phones and social accounts before heading for the cabin.

"No—""Yes!" Chris and Sabrina said at the same time.

"Great. I'll come with."

Chris scowled but said nothing. They joined the passengers on the moving ramp that led to the city surface. Sabrina gave a half-skip to fall in step with Mik.

"Where've you been?" she asked.

"Just staying away from the house. Your mom's having a cleaning frenzy. I think she likes not having robots—gives her something to do."

"Mom's got plenty to do—" Chris said defiantly.

Sabrina broke in. "Her type A is showing, now that she's off work."

Mik grinned. "Yeah, what's the deal with that? She get canned?"

"Just suspended," Chris corrected him.

"And they call me the black sheep," Mik dug at him. "Ron does anyhow, and I get the feeling Mom agrees with him. At least, they don't seem interested in finding me. I'll bet Grandma and Grandpa miss my ass," he added. "And Aunt Jen and your dad must think I'm alright, or they wouldn't have done all this. I hope they can afford this new place. Now that she's out of work."

"She's on paid leave," Chris corrected again.

"They won't fire her," Sabrina said with certainty. "She's got all kinds of valuable knowledge nobody else has."

"Oh, yeah?"

To Chris's horror, his sister took the bait.

Sabrina bragged, "She's working on this breakthrough intelligence technology. It's all very hush-hush." She caught Chris's glare. "So? Mik's family. He won't tell. And Mom's stuff is… *Mom's* stuff. Not mine," she said, tossing her long lock over a shoulder. She'd let her blonde hair grow out naturally.

"Brin," Chris said between gritted teeth. "You promised."

"Promised what?" Mik asked.

Chris reached over and put a hand on his sister's mouth, stopping her in her tracks. She angrily brushed him away.

"Never *mind*," Chris said, raising his voice. "It's none of your business."

"What's none of my business?" When his cousin went mum, Mik repeated the query a few times, hoping annoyance would pry something else loose.

It worked.

"It's none of our business too," Sabrina complained. "Mom won't tell us all the details, but it has something to do with Maxi coming alive. Arctic, huh?"

Chris's expression told Mik that this information was priceless.

"Totally," he said.

>>> <<<

Jennifer bided her time, though not patiently, as her administrative leave dragged on. After two weeks, the opportunity she was looking for arrived: the Peace Week holiday. The Ethics lab at OC-4 would be all but deserted, and she'd need every advantage possible just to get in the door.

Ruby and Rip expected Jennifer's family to visit like they did at this time every year. But their daughter phoned to say she was sick and would have to postpone the trip. Lying did not come easily to Jennifer Peterson. The guilt amplified as she gave her children the opposite excuse— that a bug was running through the family in Harmony. She hoped that by the time anyone found her out, she'd have completed her… errand.

At the apex of her guilty conscience, though, lay her decision to keep her husband in the dark about her intentions, as well. If she were caught in criminal trespass and theft, and if George knew about it, he could be found complicit. Jesus, she loved him. She knew he would understand… even after all she'd put him through recently. And all she was about to put him through.

She added another falsehood to the list on the Monday evening that kicked off Peace Week by saying she had a project she wanted to finish at the glassblowing studio. She asked George to take the kids to the big street fair on OC-1 for music and fireworks. The family typically missed the celebration when they traveled to Montana.

"Sure," George said easily. "It'll be fun. I'm not wild to repeat my commute on vacation, but sure. I saw the bots building the grandstands yesterday."

After dinner, Jennifer kissed George, synced up Maxi, and left the cabin.

En route to the underground, Jennifer's fake composure crumbled. *I don't even have a plan!* she berated herself, knees buckling. Maxi, trotting beside her, tilted her head up at her mistress. The dog's gray eyes offered a virtual steadiness, almost a shoulder to lean on. *Okay,* Jennifer thought. *This is no time to freak. I've come too far.*

Inside the bus crowded with vacationers, she set the dog on her lap and felt a tenuous calm settle over her. She reined in her thoughts to within the here and now. Idly, she wondered if the developers of robotic pets had replicated the feature in live animals that lowered humans' blood pressure through proximity and a sense of companionship. It felt like it.

But that comfort fell away the closer they got to OC-4.

Tension crept into Jennifer's bones as she and Maxi left the underground for the surface plaza in front of the WLC office complex. She hadn't been back since James Ting had released her from the boardroom that night. When she asked how long it would be before she could resume work, he'd said simply, "I'll let ya know." Jennifer wasn't sure she'd make it past the front door guard, let alone into the most secure area of the Ethics compound. She looked down at Maxi, who walked slightly ahead of her, to ground herself in why the hell she was doing this.

Trust.

The syllable rang in her ears, and she mentally repeated the word with each footstep as she approached the entrance. The panel sensors admitted the public to the lobby, so Jennifer wasn't surprised to be let into the building. But there stood the guard robot, a golden, pillar-shaped security device with a speech protocol, a facial-recognition system... and an iris scanner that detected security clearance levels.

"Good evening, Ms. Peterson," the guard welcomed her. "I see you've brought Maxi."

Jennifer nearly choked with apprehension. She gave her pet a sidelong glance. Now what?

Let me.

Jennifer hesitated, then felt her initiative shift to Maxi. The energy surge made the miniature Aussie appear to grow in stature. The lights on her collar, once just red and blue, pulsed in a rainbow of colors. Jennifer could practically feel charged electrons bouncing off the walls. What was happening? In a flash, Jennifer understood. Maxi was accessing the main database!

The holographic displays in the entry hall flickered and the dog collar lights glowed brightly as the robotic pet hacked into the building's system. Jennifer tamped down a sick feeling, expecting a blast of sirens and a wave of police drones to respond to the violation. Instead, the security gate swung open automatically.

She and Maxi lurched through.

"Have a nice day!" the guard called after her.

Jennifer took the open-platform elevator down three levels to the sub-basement, where valuables were secured. She never had been cleared for access here and wondered what to do next. *Guess I'll just use the Force,* she thought grimly, walking blindly down the hall. She took a chance, and turned left at a dead-end "T."

Jennifer heard a commotion, and quickly backpedaled. A door hissed closed. Voices grew louder, coming her way. Before she remembered that she hadn't set the Mute command, Maxi gave two sharp barks.

"What's a dog doing loose down here?" came a male voice that could've been either human or humanesque.

Jennifer backed up against the wall and froze. Beads of sweat formed a headband at her temples.

"Doubt it's got lockbox permissions," came a reply, followed by chuckles.

This was the place! But they—men or bots—were coming toward her.

Just then, Maxi pulled away and put on the juice. She scampered right for whomever was in the hall, taking a left at the "T"—and then, presumably, shooting past them, for Jennifer heard cries of "Hey!" and "Hold on!"

Instinctively, she reached for her bracelet and tapped it. So much for the Follow Me command. *It's only a dozen years of work on four legs. She'll come back.* She let out a silent, deep breath and moved forward, angling left at the end of the hallway.

Sure enough, there was the secure depository, actually so labeled. But the door had automatically closed and locked when the last visitors had left.

Damn! What she wouldn't give for an old-fashioned skeleton key. Only the proper iris pattern that corresponded to a clearance list would free the door panel. *And that, I ain't got.* Fortunately, despair had fled with the rise of endorphins and cortisol in Jennifer's bloodstream. She put her mind to the problem. What else would disable the building's lock system? *Think!*

She could call in a bomb threat. That would add one more count to the list of felonies she was compiling. Fire? All she needed was a phalanx of firefighter bots descending on the sub-basement.

Just then, Maxi came scurrying back from the other direction, her collar lights showing their normal reds and blues. She planted herself in front of Jennifer and gave two more yips. Trying to decipher this, Jennifer hoped for the same ploy that had worked with the entry guard.

The door remained frozen.

Maybe the dog's eye would unlock it. Jennifer scooped her up and faced the sensor. Nothing. Perhaps she'd depleted her energy stores.

Suddenly, Maxi gave a strong twist and thrust, and burst from Jennifer's arms. She yipped again and dodged forward, giving her mistress a nip on the calf.

"Okay! I'll try."

But she was afraid to let the scanner photograph her eye. That might bring all hell down on her, and good luck trying to escape from the depths of the basement. Warily, Jennifer waved her left hand in front of the sensor.

Click! Hiss.…

The panel parted. Her electronic bracelet must have triggered something—maybe a redial of the previous visitor's eye scan.

Who cared? She and Maxi shot inside to find a vault filled with rows of stacked, numbered compartments.

If only Jennifer knew which one held the biomedical samples… and among those, which one would actually complete the relevant neural circuits. Then another ugly thought entered her mind: were these drawers booby-trapped to ward off thieves such as herself?

Again, the internal suggestion rang out.

Trust.

Jennifer pushed on a compartment face... and it noiselessly slid open.

A row of delicate glass and silver cylinders stood neatly in a holder. She put her hand on first one, then another. *Oh, the hell with it!* She took them all, and the compartment slid shut.

Jennifer glanced a Maxi for validation. The dog just turned and moved for the door. Jennifer hid the evidence in a shoulder bag she was carrying.

The pair backtracked through the building, Jennifer's heart pounding so hard she thought it would burst. A panicked notion that she might be holding its replacement in her bag brought an incongruous smile. She took a service ramp instead of the elevator and emerged at the far end of the entrance lobby. She was running now, and Maxi bounded several paces in front of her, the dog's claws and Jennifer's footfalls producing towering echoes in the high-ceilinged chamber.

Their movement was picked up by building sensors, which activated two nearby mobile security robots. Like self-propelled luggage, they locked onto Jennifer's course and followed her, requesting a security scan. The broadcast echoed in the empty hall.

Desperation fueled acceleration. When Jennifer ignored command, the two gold, eyeless bots issued a second warning: "Stop! Present security credentials within thirty seconds or we will issue a building-wide security lockdown!"

Jennifer kept going, but threw a glance over her shoulder. Maxi blocked the bots, her collar showing its prism of lights more faintly.

"Fifteen seconds!"

Jennifer ran back to the spot, ready to grab Maxi. If they couldn't escape, she might have time to erase her files—but she might have to damage the dog to do it.

"Ten… nine…"

Jennifer braced herself and reached for her pet. Just then, the collar lights grew more intense. She backed off as Maxi seemed to enlarge once more, projecting a palpable energy.

The holographic displays around them and the lights in the lobby flickered.

"Eight…"

Jennifer waited. There was no seven. The hall went silent. The bots slowed, then fell motionless as some unseen force deactivated them.

Maxi barked and feinted toward the door.

Jennifer clutched at her shoulder bag. "Let's go!"

She and the dog took off running again. They leapt the waist-high lobby gate, and the door guard said, "Have a good evening, Ms. Peterson!"

The last thing Jennifer thought before they blew out the front door was, *I'd better be right.*

CHAPTER 17

Jennifer reached home a little after seven o'clock. George and the kids wouldn't be back for hours. There should be plenty of time to work on the implants... that was, if nobody had learned of the department security breach.

"Come on, Maxi!" Jennifer led her pet to the work room that she and George shared in the cabin and ramped up the lighting. She carefully unwrapped the cylinders she'd taken from the bag, hoping everything was still intact.

The receptacles were each marked with a string of QR codes that meant nothing to Jennifer. Inside were minute devices that might replace or interface with any number of human body parts. Did one of them contain a brain-computer link? If it did, how would she implant the thing in Maxi's body? *I'm not a damn neurosurgeon!* Jennifer felt her confidence sliding away, like loose mercury over a kitchen floor.

Let me help.

She met Maxi's gray eyes, which fixed on her intently. The dog seemed to be willing her to let down her guard, to stop trying to control what was out of her grasp. Jennifer fought this urge. She was the one who had begun this saga. She had enlisted George, back before they were married, when they were both still at Stanford, wrestling to pin down the factors that would fuse ethics and intelligence, world economics with social justice. Or was it George who had drawn her to his way of thinking?

One of their late-night debates returned to her now, a friendly argument that had taken place on their usual stage, the bench under the tree outside of Landau Hall. Jennifer had been advocating for full government backing of unbridled artificial-intelligence research. "The boundaries are limitless, Xical," she'd said. "We need to be freed from the politics and purse-strings that would hobble the science."

George had taken a more prudent tack. "But, we don't know where that research will lead. Powerful forces—moneyed forces, military forces—will want to use that science for dark ends. We must be sure that it leads us up, toward the light."

"And how would you propose we do that?"

"Systematically. Humanely. With one foot on moral ground."

"But that will only hold the research back! We need wings, not brakes. We should let advancement set its own pace."

"But not its own course," he protested.

That dispute had ended inconclusively, as neither of them would give in. But little by little, Jennifer recalled, their sentiments had converged. She hadn't wanted to see a superhuman intelligence stripped of mitigating emotion.

And George had sought an end to the petty quibbles and divisions of man that seemed to prevent its higher evolution.

So, here she was, at the nexus of it all—she had the data, she had the ethical framework. All that remained was the unifying piece that would bring it all together. It was her victory to realize. It was her baby. And, she had to admit, she had no idea what to do next.

Let go.

She stared at Maxi, looking into, then past, the gray depths of her eyes. Letting go was not part of Jennifer's skill set. This shortcoming had tripped her up from time to time, and had become her greatest detriment in raising her kids. Her yearning for control had probably created Sabrina's early rebellious streak, and may have made poor Chris too dependent. The years managing others in the lab had only added to her bent. A need to command was so much a part of her that it might have been biological, implanted at the cellular level. If she couldn't take charge, who was she?

"How am I supposed to let all this go?" she said out loud.

For a long moment, nothing came to mind. Jennifer's vision lost focus as frustration closed in. Defeat seemed to creep up behind it.

Then Maxi gave a whimper and brought her back to the present.

What would George do?

Dutifully, Jennifer turned her thoughts to the question. George Xical was a brilliant problem solver. As a lieutenant-secretary of Citizen Welfare, he had jumped hurdle after hurdle to bring the Core government within reach of its official mission points meant to foster wealth sharing. But, Jennifer knew, he rarely started out with the right solution. He brainstormed and debated and collected opposing viewpoints. He weighed the consequences and considered alternatives. It wasn't merely his intellect that drove him in the right direction. He'd told her he did his best work during meditation. *He let go*, she realized.

Jennifer took a slow, deep breath. She unfurled the fists that she hadn't realized were so tightly coiled. The rest of her muscles began to relax—in her toes, at her knees, her hips. Her rib cage dropped. Her shoulders rolled back. An invisible wisp of smoke rose from her spinal cord through her neck, and out the top of her head.

At last, there was nothing.

Something inside made her dismiss the panic. Made her let go, and rest there.

After a time, she heard a noise. *Oooh-ooo, oooh-ooo!* whined Maxi from the floor.

Suddenly, Jennifer knew what came next.

Never mind which test tube held the right part! Never mind where that interface belonged. She'd let Maxi figure it out.

The robot was not a live animal; it couldn't be carved open, its brain exposed. There were only two ways to get inside: through the face plate, and through the ear canal. Something told Jennifer that a cochlear implant was the best bet.

She retrieved a pair of smartglasses that would let her view the dozen or so tiny devices she'd taken from the lockbox, plus a pair of jewelers forceps that she'd lifted from the lab for working on Maxi's memory chips. Her composure flooded back in. This, she thought, must be how George's mind worked—by giving itself the space and time to make the right connections.

One of these was a precaution that would allow for direct transfer of the dog's files. She had nearly lost them all back at the Ethics building. A few more seconds and she would've had to destroy them—all her work, all that information… all that hope. She nudged her pet for assistance and fished in the collection of bioparts for a cortical device she could place in her own earpiece—one that would convert digital files to audio and transmit them. In this manner, Jennifer would gain a wireless link between herself and her robotic dog, allowing information to pass from brain to brain.

With intuition, or Maxi's pure energy force, as her guide, she chose a likely apparatus and fumbled with her earpiece, eventually satisfied that she'd inserted it properly. Whether it would work was anybody's guess.

Jennifer had just lifted Maxi up onto one of the work tables when the telephone rang. *Shit! Should I answer it?* She nearly let the call go to old-fashioned voicemail, but realized it would be better to answer as though nothing special was happening. She picked up the hardwired extension.

"Peterson!" It was James Ting. "What the fucking hell is going on?" He no longer sounded like her trusting boss.

"Building Inventory recorded your visit. I had the cameras checked. What the hell were you doing at Ethics? What were you doing in Biostorage?"

Jennifer's muscles went rigid. They'd caught her and Maxi on film—there was no time to fabricate anything remotely plausible.

"I'm giving you five seconds to explain yourself. Then I'm calling CDE."

Jennifer's brain whirred. He'd unleash Core Data Enforcement no matter what she said. She hung up, then immediately dialed another number. After a quick talk, she dialed George.

Fortunately, he never left the island without his phone. *Please pick up, please pick up....*

"Xical here."

Jennifer blurted into the mouthpiece, "George. There's no time to explain. I'm—we're in deep shit. We've got to get out of the country!"

"What th'—?"

She cut him off. "Bring the kids to the South Land Transit Station and wait there for me. I'll be driving Laura's four-by-four."

He tried to wrap his mind around this. "What about travel papers... ?"

"There's no time to head north. We'll have to risk the Idaho border. We've got to make it to Dad's farm—we'll be safe there!"

Again, she cut off his questions. Time was running out.

Maxi lay obediently on the table, the hinged panel atop her head open to offer access to one ear. Jennifer slid the smartglasses over her eyes and, as quickly as she dared, began transferring the bio implants from the protective tubes to Maxi's ear canal. Now that the moment of truth had arrived, neither her hands—nor her resolve—wavered.

>>> <<<

Mik waited until Jennifer had broken the telephone connection. Then he slowly replaced the extension receiver in Chris's bedroom. This was all he needed to know. He slipped out of the cabin and walked briskly down the path toward the Buzz Zone islet. It would be safer to call Ron from there.

Earlier in the evening, when Jennifer had left the house, Mik had tagged after her. Her story about doing some glassblowing instead of joining the rest of her family for fun at the fireworks display sounded a bit off. When she got on the bus to OC-4 instead of OC-3, he knew he was onto something. Fortunately, the public transport was stuffed with fairgoers. He had easily blended into the crowd at the back of her car and on the way up the surface ramp.

They arrived at a blocky building with an official designation: WESTERN LAND CORE DEPARTMENT OF ETHICS. His blood raced as his aunt and Maxi went inside.

He didn't entertain any questions. What they were doing wasn't as important as the fact that they weren't supposed to be there—of that, Mik was sure. Several of his contacts would be interested in this information. But it would help if he had more specifics, and, if he stuck with her, Mik was certain they would come to light.

That gamble had paid off; the phone conversation confirmed it. Now he had a destination as well as the route she intended. He could probably peddle this news to more than one interested party.

He hurried into the Buzz Zone, grabbed his phone from the charger, and went to the work station to see who among his contacts was online. He lifted the corner of his mouth, satisfied. The night was just beginning.

>>> <<<

Finishing her work on Maxi, Jennifer helped the dog jump down from the table and then barged through the house, grabbing supplies. Who knew when they'd be back? There was no time to bask in success, or even evaluate the job to make sure it had succeeded. A quick glance at Maxi told her nothing. The pet didn't look any different, and no helpful thought transmissions were forthcoming.

The sun was sinking into the western horizon in an ocean of orange and red when she and Maxi left the cabin by the back door. Something prodded Jennifer to fade into the cedar hedge that lined the main pathway toward the city center. She did, and Maxi followed. The next moment, the sound of sirens surged in the distance. Ting had probably sicced CDE on her. But another conveyance was coming her way—a black truck that resembled an armored jeep. The occupants must have had special authorization, since motor vehicles weren't normally allowed in this sector.

She let it pass in the direction of the cabin, then moved on again as fast as she could, finally emerging at the end of the hedge. There, a narrower walking path formed a shortcut to the transportation garage. No vehicle could follow them here.

Waiting for a bus would have wasted valuable minutes. Instead, Jennifer decided to risk taking her own vehicle for the trip out of town and hope it wasn't identified. Just having Maxi by her side steadied her. She threw her belongings in the backseat, let the dog sit up front, got in the driver's side, and took off.

"We're gonna make it, girl," she said, as though the robotic pet needed reassurance instead of herself. Maxi sat quietly and did not respond.

Jennifer drove to the outskirts of the Seattle metro area, met briefly with Laura, and switched vehicles. Her friend told her the four-wheel-drive had at least ten hours' charge in it—enough to make a beeline dash for the WLC border, but not enough to get all the way through Idaho's panhandle and western Montana. Maybe Grant could meet them somewhere. Jennifer resolved to worry about that later.

She thrust her attention on traffic, as the self-driving option wasn't available on backroads. Inching through the congestion around the transportation hub at OC-1, Jennifer didn't immediately spot George and the kids where she'd told them to wait. *Holy shit!* she thought impatiently. This was no time for Chris to wander off or for Sabrina to throw a tantrum. Then the crowd at the south station parted, and she saw George searching anxiously down the street. He recognized her at the wheel of the red SUV and called over his shoulder. The kids popped around a corner and followed him to the car.

"Get in!" Jennifer gestured for George to take Maxi on his lap and for Chris and Sabrina to sit in back. With the doors still closing, she hit the accelerator.

No one dared ask the first question. Jennifer reached over and squeezed George's hand, and urged the vehicle onto a state highway, away from the setting sun and into the gathering dusk.

CHAPTER 18

Thank god it was September and not even a month later, Jennifer said to herself. There would be snow falling anytime now in the forests and foothills of Mount Baker, which the state road bisected on its way east. The route between here and Harmony crossed two more mountain ranges, plus swathes of high desert. The upper-elevation passes would soon be draped in white.

"Mom, how come you don't take the interstate?" Chris wanted to know.

Jennifer didn't answer, just kept driving.

Sabrina, after carping about missing the fireworks, had decided to take the trip as a lark. "I love Wenatchee," she said, meaning the national forest they were traveling through, named for a local Indian tribe. Their headlights flashed on a fall freshet that poured off a slope at the roadside. "No fireworks, but at least there's waterfalls," she said.

Jennifer was afraid to break the spell and start explaining herself. But more than an hour into the run, she could feel George's patience about to shatter. She glanced at him in the passenger's seat. He held Maxi tight and looked back at Jennifer, his eyes two dark hollows in the dim car interior.

"I love you," Jennifer said softly. Then she began to recount the evening's events, speaking as if George were the only one in earshot. But, the further she got into the details, the less she wanted to reveal—and the more insistent the quizzing from the backseat became.

Chris let fear overtake his excitement at the unplanned road trip. "Are the cops after us?"

Jennifer looked at George. "Yes."

"Did you take something from the glass studio?" Sabrina asked, fully confused.

Jennifer felt a pang; the girl had believed her excuse, probably all of her excuses. "No—I took something else. From work."

George asked quietly, "Is it what I think it is?"

Now Jennifer kept her eyes on the patch of road illuminated by their headlights. "Yes."

It was George's turn to reach out and squeeze her on the forearm. "Oh, my god, Jen. Did you… ?"

She nodded, and he squeezed her again, so hard it hurt. She could tell he was both elated and terrified.

Sabrina took all this in, and put two and two together. Her voice traveled from behind the passenger's seat: "Does this have something to do with Maxi?"

George answered for his wife. "You bet it does!" He appealed to Jennifer to tell them more—everything. "They're old enough to know, sweetheart."

He was right.

Jennifer had to backtrack in her story, first, though; without knowing the signs of Maxi's growing intelligence, her rash moves tonight would seem crazy, selfish, or worse.

She reminded them of Maxi's off-program performance at the agility trials.

"We knew about that, Mom," Sabrina said. "I got blamed for cheating on her program, but all I did was follow Maxi around the course. She's the one who learned it."

"Touché," Jennifer said. "It was that leap, from obeying commands to outright self-direction that told me we were getting somewhere." She explained how she believed a saturation point of select information was the stepping stone to a higher intelligence—one that could reason for itself.

"But I thought a supreme consciousness was just a science fiction myth," practical Chris surmised. "Or, if it was possible, it wouldn't happen for several more lifetimes."

"It feels like I've aged that much," George put in wryly.

"Well, theory begets reality, sometimes," Jennifer pointed out. *In other words, I was right.* God, it felt good to finally acknowledge that. Although the victory might be short-lived.

She went on to describe the need for bioidentical tissue that would allow Maxi to utilize the information the way a human brain would.

"You mean, you found the proper brain-computer interface in that box of tricks you broke into?" George clarified.

"I found... I'm not sure what I found. But I went ahead and implanted everything, hoping that the neural interface was in there." Jennifer didn't mention that Maxi, herself, had suggested doing that. "Maxi's not a real dog or a real person—so any redundancy was less likely to do her harm."

"Did it?" Sabrina asked worriedly.

Jennifer hesitated. "We... don't know, hon." Maxi had been quiet and only minimally responsive since the procedure. In fact, she'd done nothing outside of her dog program boundaries.

"Well?" Chris asked the next obvious question. "Did it *work*?"

"I'm—not sure," Jennifer had to admit.

"Holy crap, Jennifer," George muttered. "We're running from the law, and you don't know if you even—"

"I did my best!" she cried, and the tension finally overcame her. She checked the rearview mirror, then hauled the wheel to the right and let the car bump to a stop on the shoulder. She slumped forward, hitting the horn and making all of them jump.

"You need to rest," George said, more calmly. "Let me drive awhile."

The two of them got out of the car and met in front of the hood. George embraced Jennifer, kissing the top of her head and burrowing his face in her short hair. "Whatever you did, my love, I'm so proud of you. So proud."

George took over and pushed the car into the night, along the now-empty highway that led through eastern Washington, toward the old city of Spokane and the little towns along the Washington-Idaho line. These communities in the dry steppes of the state had all but cleared out with the Earth's warming trend. This time of year, though, the area was bearable. George pressed down on the accelerator and let the vehicle eat up some of the flat, vacant road before they hit mountains again.

The kids dozed off for a time. They must have felt George's and Jennifer's apprehension rising, though, as the car approached the Idaho border.

Sabrina sat up and asked sleepily, "Mom? How about Mik? Did you tell him where we were going?"

She admitted that she had not. "I assumed he was out with friends. There was no time to track him down." To herself, she confessed that her nephew had not even entered her mind, until now.

Chris had awakened, and his sister's interest in their cousin's whereabouts brought back her previous disclosure. "You know, Mom, Sabrina may have given Mik a little too much information when we were talking last week."

"What's that, hon?" Her troubled nephew had seemed oblivious to most things regarding the family recently, since he had taken up with that bunch of friends. "Information about what?"

Chris exchanged glances with his sister and, against her silent wishes, continued. "About Maxi."

>>> <<<

George Xical maneuvered the SUV to Spokane, and then followed the state highway north, to avoid merging with the interstate. He'd been a vagabond before, in his younger years as a beach bum, but he'd never been a fugitive. Although Jennifer hadn't said so, there might well be more sinister people on their tails than the police. The prospect made his insides itch, as though his organs were scraping against one another. His children had been thrown into grave danger—his wife might go to prison. These possibilities were worse than anything that might befall him.

And yet, he could not condemn Jennifer for their predicament. He had, after all, sanctioned her research over the decades—had known, somewhere deep inside, that it might not all end in sweetness and light. Perhaps they had lulled themselves into false confidence in pursuing what they believed to be the moderating effects of ethical behavior and social justice. He couldn't regret that, although at present, it did seem somewhat naive.

If only we could stay right here, right now—just travel forever through nowhere, never arriving, just being together. This rare lapse of wishful thinking was necessarily brief. The highway jutted eastward, bringing them within a few miles of the international boundary.

Jennifer must have been thinking about it too. She shifted Maxi on her lap and leaned for the glovebox. She drew out a small object. George caught its dim reflected outline in the passenger window—it was a pistol. He gave his wife a wordless nod of recognition.

"Pull over a sec, George," she said. "I'd better try to call Grant from here, before we lose a cell signal. There should still be service from Spokane."

They took a brief telephone and outdoor bathroom break, and resumed their trek.

Out here, away from any urban lights, the night was lonely and black. George hit the brights, which shone a few yards ahead of them. As the family rode in tense silence, the only sound came from the rubber tires against the asphalt. Then the headlights picked out a brown road sign: LEAVING WASHINGTON. There was no WLC checkpoint on this byway, but ahead stood a series of wooden billboards announcing the Ameristates border and the many penalties for crossing it unlawfully.

"Abandon hope, all ye who enter," George murmured.

The car passed these markers uneventfully, almost in defiance of the warnings and threats. George felt his forearms relax a hair against the steering wheel. *You never know what you'll get at the border,* he thought. The next second, he regretted the notion. Headlights swung into the lane behind them.

Just play it cool, he told himself, glancing at Jennifer, who held the pistol beneath Maxi on her lap. They had reached another mountainous area. Lights flashed in and out of the rearview mirror as the car behind them rounded the curves just after their vehicle did. The highway followed the Clark Fork river, through forests and watersheds popular with hikers and campers, though tourists were not plentiful this late in the season. George saw a sign beckoning anglers to the trout habitat at Lake Pend Oreille and decided it was time to see how persistent their followers were going to be. He cut off on a side road that led to one of the campgrounds. When the headlights didn't reappear, he pulled over gently and cut his own lights.

"Dad—?"

"Shh!"

They waited thirty seconds, a minute, two more. George sat until Maxi began to whine, ever so softly, from Jennifer's lap. The mirrors did not reveal any more headlights.

George pulled back onto the access road, and then returned to the highway, headed north.

>>> <<<

Jennifer squeezed Maxi's sides and roughed up her fur. They had reached familiar territory in western Montana, where the highway sliced through the mountains of the national park, not far from their usual Canadian border entrance. The moon had set, but night was fading. Soon, sparks of dawn would light the way toward Harmony—toward home.

Unless there was any gas in the hybrid, they wouldn't make it much farther, especially since the road rose and fell and doubled back around this section of the Rockies. She'd instructed Grant to find whatever means of transport he could and make his way west along Route 2, until he found them.

It won't be much of a guessing game, she thought. There was literally no one else on the road—or, at least, no one to be seen. They were close enough to the international line that company men could be roaming this way. On the other hand, they were closing in on Blackfeet territory. Jennifer knew that the inhabitants of the Indian reservation had tolerated travelers in the past. But the crossing stations were closed overnight, and she'd never tried to pass through this late. Or was it early?

An eerie calm permeated the predawn hour. Maxi roused, then settled back on Jennifer's numb thighs.

"Mom?"

"Yeah, Chris."

"I'm… really glad you finished your research. I hope it turns out alright."

"Me, too. I guess you could say, it's about time."

"I'm happy for you too," Sabrina piped up. "We know how much you wanted this."

Well, then, it must have all been worth it, Jennifer thought ruefully. Committing a felony, losing my job, absconding with minors, crossing international lines… *Small price to pay.*

Something flashed in the sideview mirror. She noticed a pair of lights whiz up behind them.

"Just keep going," she told George.

The road had cut out of the forested foothills and onto the high plains. Jennifer checked the time; it was 6:32, on the cusp of first light. *Thank goodness,* she thought, not that it mattered whether the sun shone or not, at this point. She felt Maxi's smooth coat beneath her fingers. Everything of consequence in her life was inside this car.

George hit a pothole and swore. The road had grown increasingly rough the closer they'd come to the reservation. You could bet that Grubb's federal dollars weren't finding their way into construction budgets here. Just then, the car gave a grinding sound and slowed.

George pressed the accelerator, but it didn't pick up any speed.

He looked over at his wife. "I think we're almost out of kryptonite."

The lights behind them grew brighter.

"Maybe we can get a charge, or ask about a tow," Jennifer said.

"Let's see." George hit the brakes and put the car in Park. Then he opened the door and got out.

Instead of slowing, the jeep behind them accelerated. Shouts came from its open windows. A shot rang out, the sound of a high-powered rifle.

The family were sitting ducks on the flat, open tarmac. George ducked back inside the car and threw the transmission in gear.

"Get out of here, Dad!" Chris yelled.

The jeep bore down on them, closer now.

Their SUV careened down the road until George spied a thicket of conifers up ahead, off to one side. He yanked the wheel, and they left the asphalt and jolted over hard, rocky ground.

Jennifer felt her teeth rattle. She clutched Maxi close. "Hold on, kids!"

They reached the bank of a creek that sustained the grove of trees and some tangled underbrush, George screeched to a stop. "Chris! Sabrina! Out of the car." He threw a wild look at his wife. "Jen! Go with them. Run! These guys'll follow me."

She stared into his eyes in the early, gray dawn, but just for an instant.

"Go!"

Jennifer handed him the pistol. Then she heaved open the door, dropped Maxi to the ground, and tore off after the children, deeper into the trees.

Breath, footsteps, and a sense of doom throbbed in Jennifer's ears. "Run, kids!" She slipped on a patch of moist earth and nearly fell. Maxi backtracked, barking.

Had their pursuers followed George? Would he be able to outrun them?

Just then, Jennifer heard the tread of heavy boots on the hard ground behind her, coming fast. She screamed, "Run, Chris! Sabrina—!"

Another shot fired. This time, Jennifer thought she felt as well as heard it.

The wind sucked from her lungs, and she staggered. She could not even cry out.

Still, every sense was crystal clear. She felt the blood pulse in her temples and wrists. She smelled sharp spruce scent in the air. She heard yells and yips ahead of her on the trail, and behind her... nothing. The footsteps had faded. Whoever had tracked her must have been satisfied with scaring her half to death.

Then she noticed a warmth and dampness down the front of her shirt. The rising light around her revealed a dark stain spreading outward, too deliberately to have come from a puddle splash or falling rain.

Maxi bounded back up the path, with Chris and Sabrina right behind her.

Sabrina screamed.

Chris's voice went husky. "Mom..." He ran to her and held her, half upright, where she'd fallen.

A dizzying wave hit Jennifer, but it wasn't a break with consciousness. Maxi pushed against her, and now Jennifer felt a deep pain inside—the pain of loss, the pain of… unfulfillment. All the years, all the work and waiting, gone to dust.

Weakly, she said, "I've failed you…."

Sabrina was crying. "No, you didn't."

But it was Maxi that Jennifer meant, or the seed of power that was inside of Maxi.

Let me help.

"Kids—"

"Shh, Mom," Chris gripped her shoulders. "Don't… Save your breath. We'll—go get Dad."

A proverbial second wind flowed through Jennifer, and she looked into Chris's sweet face. She could make out his gray eyes in the dawn. "Your father… will be fine. He's a master of the wilderness."

"Isn't there something we can do?" Sabrina implored.

Jennifer kept still.

Yes.

But, what?

Unleash me. Unlock me.

Jennifer looked into Maxi's eyes, and then at Sabrina's and Chris's. "My babies…" She held out a hand to Sabrina, who drew close. The three of them huddled together. "It's… up to you," Jennifer said. "First Chris. Then you, Sabrina." Her voice was dwindling. "Iris scan…" It drifted off.

Chris grew frantic. "What, Mom? What about it?" He began to sob.

Come to me.

Sabrina heard her mother's voice... but it was in her own ears. It wanted her to—suddenly, the girl knew what to do.

Maxi left Jennifer's side and planted herself in front of her mistress's daughter. Sabrina knelt down and let the dog capture her gaze. "Chris!"

But he was fixated on their mother, his sobs coughing out in spasms.

"Chris!"

Come to me.

Now he heard a voice that wasn't Sabrina's—it was Jennifer's voice, resonating inside his head. But she hadn't spoken. Sabrina grabbed his hands and forced him to look her in the face.

To Chris's wonder, her eyes, once gray like his, now shone a deep, violet-blue, broken with light and dark flecks, like a flower petal's. She thrust her chin at Maxi, and Chris obliged. He opened his eyes wide, looked firmly into Maxi's, then squeezed them closed.

The whole world seemed to have stopped. But when Chris lifted his lids, wet with tears, Sabrina saw the gray was gone, and the rich dark-chocolate shade of George's irises was now reflected in her brother's.

"Mom!" Sabrina said, hauling Chris over to where their mother lay.

Jennifer saw immediately what had happened. "Aren't you two beautiful?" she whispered.

Then her voice, louder and stronger, rang out. It seemed to encircle Maxi, whose ice-blue eyes held a gift of knowledge, and not a little humor.

I am not this body anymore.

Chris propped Jennifer up so she could see. Their onetime pet, no longer a mere collection of circuitry and hardware, projected an aura of light and color. The rainbow of lights on her collar glowed and sparkled. She spoke. The voice that filled the air was Jennifer's—the voice and sensibility that she knew best.

Feebly, Jennifer raised a hand and touched her earpiece. White-hot light radiated from it. It grew stronger and stronger, taking on a copper hue. Meanwhile, Jennifer's gaze seemed to fix on some far-off pleasantry. The earpiece and Maxi's collar both shone brightly at once, and then the earpiece gave a *pop!* and blew. Instead of pain, the fusion brought release.

As Jennifer's vision faded, her essence grew. Chris felt it. Sabrina felt it.

Before their eyes, a perfect body projected from Maxi's collar, encasing them all in light—like the atoms of a star, or a glass globe—formed without gravity, without outlines, without limits. In the midst of their anguish, Chris and Sabrina were filled with a sense of certainty, a feeling of unity they had never known before.

Now Jennifer felt it too. She hadn't failed. She felt the transference of her mind, absorbed by a force of infinite possibilities. Her love was boundless. Her lifetime was just beginning.

About the Author

Ben Way is a best selling author, leading futurologist, technologist, inventor, and entrepreneur. With over twenty years of experience in technology and innovation, Ben has travelled the world seeking out and developing new technologies. As a leading voice on the challenges and benefits of tomorrow's technology, he has advised some of the world's leading institutions, including the White House, regarding technological preparations for the future. He is the recipient of the millennium entrepreneur of the year award and has appeared on numerous technology and philanthropy television programs, as well as presenting Bright Young Wonders on Robotics.

Also by the Author

JOBOCALYPSE

A look at the rapidly changing face of robotics and how it will revolutionize employment and jobs over the next thirty years. Ben Way lays out the arguments in favor of and against the mechanization of our society, as well as the amazing advantages and untold risks, as we march into this ever-present future.